Enid Blyton's

A BOOK OF
PIXIE STORIES

First published 1989
Reprinted 1990

Published by Dean, an imprint of
The Hamlyn Publishing Group Limited,
Michelin House,
81 Fulham Road,
London SW3 6RB,
England

Text copyright © Darrell Waters Limited 1950,
1951, 1952, 1953, 1954, 1955

Enid Blyton is a registered trademark of Darrell Waters Limited

Illustrations copyright © The Hamlyn Publishing Group Limited 1989

ISBN 0 600 56327 8

Printed in Italy

Enid Blyton's
A BOOK OF
PIXIE STORIES

DEAN

CONTENTS

Dame Quickly's Wash-Tub

ONE day when Tickle the pixie was going home, he passed by Dame Quickly's cottage. He thought he would peep round and see what he could see. Dame Quickly often used magic spells, and it was fun to watch her.

But there was nobody in the cottage. On the table, by itself, stood something that made Tickle's eyes gleam. It was a wash-tub, a bright yellow one, as magic as could be.

Everyone knew Dame Quickly's wash-tub. You had only to put your dirty clothes in it, and say, "Alla malla, wash-tub, get to work!" and the wash-tub would swish the clothes round and round, clean them beautifully, and then wring them out and throw them on to the table.

"I wish I could borrow that wash-tub," thought Tickle, thinking of the big wash he had to do that afternoon. "What a pity Dame Quickly is out. I suppose she has gone to her sister's for the day. She always does on Monday."

He looked and looked at the wash-tub. Then he climbed in at the window and picked it up.

"It can't matter borrowing it," he thought. "I know I ought to ask – but if I wait till tomorrow and ask Dame Quickly, she might say no. So I'd better borrow it now. I can take it back before she comes home tonight. She won't even know I borrowed it!"

He ran off with it on his shoulders. When he got home he filled it with warm water, put some soap into the water, and then threw in all his dirty clothes and linen.

Then he tapped the tub three times and cried, "Alla, malla, wash-tub, get to work!"

And my goodness me, you should have seen that wash-tub dealing with those clothes! It swished them round and round in the soapy water and got all the dirt out as quickly as could be.

Then it tossed them out on to the table, with all the water wrung out, ready for Tickle to rinse. It was marvellous.

Tickle took them to rinse in the sink. The wash-tub made a curious whistling noise, and suddenly the curtains flew from the window and put themselves into the water. Then the wash-tub set to work on them.

"Hi!" cried Tickle. "Don't do that. Those curtains were only washed last week. Now I shall have to dry them and iron them all over again. Stop, you silly wash-tub."

But the wash-tub took no notice. It tossed the washed curtains out of the water, and then whistled again.

And into the tub jumped all the rugs and mats off the floor! It was most annoying. Tickle shouted crossly. "Will you stop behaving like this? I don't want my mats washed. Stop it, you silly wash-tub."

Out came the rugs and mats as clean as could be – and then the wash-tub whistled again. All the cushions threw themselves into the tub! But that was too much for Tickle.

"I won't have my nice feather cushions soaked with water! Now, stop it, wash-tub!"

The tub whistled again – and, oh dear, poor Tickle found himself jumping into the wash-tub too! He was swished round and round, well-soaped, squeezed, and tossed out on to the table.

"You wicked wash-tub!" he cried, wiping the soap from his eyes. "You wicked—"

The tub whistled, and into the water went Tickle again! This was a fine game, the wash-tub

thought, a very fine game indeed. It waited till Tickle had been thrown out once more, then whistled again – and in went poor Tickle, splash!

When he was tossed out for the third time he fled to the door. He ran down the road to meet Dame Quickly's bus. Oh, oh, oh, she must get her horrid wash-tub as soon as she could! Who would have thought it would behave like that?

Dame Quickly stepped off the bus. Tickle ran up to her, dripping with water.

"Dame Quickly, dear Dame Quickly, please,

please come and get your wash-tub from my house!" begged Tickle. "It is behaving so badly."

"From your house?" said Dame Quickly, in surprise. "How did my wash-tub get into your house?"

Tickle felt rather awkward. "Well, you see," he said, "I – er – I wanted to borrow it – but you were out – so I er – I – er—"

"You took it without asking!" said Dame Quickly, looking very stern. "Don't you know that's a very wrong thing to do? You knew I wouldn't lend it to you if you asked me – so you took it without asking. That's next door to stealing, you know that. You bad little pixie. Well – keep the wash-tub. I can make myself another."

"Oh!" squealed poor Tickle, "I can't keep it. I really can't. It keeps on whistling me into the water, and washing me. Oh, do, do come and get it."

Dame Quickly laughed. "What a strange lovely punishment for you," she said. "No – I tell you I don't want my tub back."

"But I shall spend the rest of my life being whistled into the water and washed!" wailed Tickle.

"That's quite likely," said Dame Quickly. "Good bye."

Tickle caught hold of her skirt, and wept big tears down his cheeks. "Please, I'll never borrow without asking again, please, I'm sorry. What can I do to show you I am sorry?"

"Ah, now you are talking properly," said Dame Quickly. "If you are really sorry, and want to make up for what you have done, I'll come and get the tub. But for the next three weeks, I shall expect you to come and do my ironing for me."

She went back to Tickle's cottage, spoke sharply to the tub, which had begun to whistle as soon as it saw Tickle again, and then put it on her shoulder.

"Now, remember," she said to Tickle, "come each Tuesday for three weeks to do my ironing. And maybe at the end of that time you will have made up your mind that it really isn't good to borrow without asking! Good-bye!"

Poor Tickle. He'll be very careful now, won't he?

The Three Wishes

ELSIE and Bobby were sitting in the meadow, and, as usual, they were quarrelling.

They were brother and sister, but to hear them quarrelling with one another, you might have thought they were enemies!

"I didn't want to come to this wood. I wanted to go up the hill," said Elsie. "You always do what you want. You never do what I want."

"Oh, you story-teller!" said Bobby. "You are the most selfish girl I know – I'm always having to do what you choose. I don't like you a bit."

"Well, I don't like—" Elsie began, and then she stopped. She had seen something moving in the buttercups near her. She put out her hand quickly and caught the thing that was moving.

To her enormous surprise, it was a pixie! The little creature gave a scream, and wriggled hard. But Elsie didn't let go. She held the little creature very tightly.

"Look!" she said to Bobby, in an excited

voice. "Look! I've caught a fairy!"

"Let me go!" squealed the little thing. "You are hurting me."

"Make her give us three wishes," said Bobby, suddenly. "Go on – tell her. We might get three wishes that would come true!"

Elsie squeezed the poor little pixie till she cried out.

"Give us three wishes and I'll let you go," she said. "Three wishes! Then we can make ourselves rich and happy and wise."

"I'll give you three wishes," said the pixie. "But they won't do you any good! Children like you can't wish for the right things! But I'll give you three wishes if you want them."

Elsie let the pixie go, and the little thing fled away among the bluebells, laughing as if she had heard a joke.

"What's she laughing at?" said Bobby. "Oh, well, never mind. Now, what shall we wish?"

"I want to wish for a budgerigar that can talk," said Elsie, at once. "I've always wanted one."

"What a silly wish!" said Bobby. "No – let's wish for a little aeroplane that will take us anywhere we want to go."

"I'm sure I don't want to fly in the air with

you as the pilot," said Elsie. "No, you're not to wish that."

"Well, I shall," said Bobby, and he wished it. "I wish I had a little aeroplane of my own, that I could fly off in."

At once a most beautiful little aeroplane flew down from the air and landed beside Bobby. He was simply delighted. He got into it and grinned at Elsie, who was very angry.

"You bad boy, to waste a wish on a thing like that!" she said, and she got up to shake him. She caught hold of his shoulders, and tried to pull him out of the aeroplane.

"I wish you were miles away!" she shouted. "You're a horrid brother to have!"

The aeroplane's engine started up, and the propeller began to whirl round. Elsie's wish was coming true!

Bobby dragged Elsie in beside him as the aeroplane flew off. "You horrid girl!" he said. "That's the second wish gone. Now goodness knows where we shall land."

They flew in the air for a long way and then the aeroplane landed on a little island. The sea splashed all round it, and except for a few strange trees and sea-birds there was nothing to be seen.

"Now see what you've done!" said Bobby. "You made us come here!" He got out of the aeroplane and walked round the little island. He came back looking gloomy.

"We can't stay here. There is nothing to eat. We should starve. We must go back home."

"How?" said Elsie.

"In the aeroplane," said Bobby. "Come on, get in. We'll fly back, and then we'll be very, very careful about what we wish for our last wish."

They got into the aeroplane – but it didn't fly off. It just stood there, its engine silent and its propeller still.

"I'm afraid we'll have to use our last wish to get back home," said Bobby, sadly. "How we have wasted them! Aeroplane, I wish you would take us back home."

The aeroplane flew up into the air and soon the children were back in the meadow again. They got out and looked at the nice little plane.

"Well, anyway, we've got an aeroplane," said Bobby. But even as he spoke the little pixie ran up, jumped into the plane, set the engine going, and flew off.

"What did I tell you?" shouted the pixie, leaning out of the aeroplane. "I said that three wishes would be wasted on children like you —and so they were! People who quarrel always do stupid things – what silly children you are!"

Bobby and Elsie watched the little aeroplane as it flew above the trees. They were very sad.

"If we hadn't quarrelled, we'd have been able to talk over what we really wanted," said Elsie. "We could have wished for some lovely things."

"Well – we will next time," said Bobby.

But there won't be a next time. Things like that don't happen twice!

It Was The Wind

TRICKY and Dob lived next door to one another. Dob was a hard-working little fellow, always busy about something. Tricky was a scamp, and he teased the life out of poor old Dob.

He undid the clothes from Dob's washing-line, so that they dropped into the mud and had to be washed all over again. He crept through a hole in his fence and took the eggs that Feathers, Dob's white hen, laid for him. He borrowed this and he borrowed that – but he always forgot to return anything.

Dob put up with Tricky and his ways very patiently, but he did wish Tricky didn't live next to him!

He didn't like Tricky at all, but he didn't tell tales of him or complain of him, so nobody ever punished Tricky or scolded him.

Still, things can't go on like that for ever, and one day a very funny thing happened.

It was an autumn day, and the leaves had blown down from the trees, spreading every-where over Dob's garden.

They were making Tricky's garden untidy, too, of course, but he didn't mind a bit. Dob *did* mind. He was a good little gardener, and he loved his garden to be tidy and neat.

So he took his broom and began to sweep his leaves into a big heap. He swept them up by the fence between his garden and Tricky's. There! Now his garden was tidy again. Dob went to fetch his barrow to put the leaves into it to take down to the rubbish-heap.

Tricky had been watching Dob sweeping up his leaves. He grinned. Here was a chance to tease Dob again, he thought. Dob had put the pile of leaves just by the hole in his fence! Tricky slipped out as soon as Dob had gone to fetch his barrow, and went to his fence.

He wriggled through the hole into the middle of the pile of leaves. Then he scattered all the leaves over the grass; what fun he was having. When he had finished, he crept back unseen through the hole.

"Dob *will* be surprised!" he thought. And Dob was. He was annoyed as well. What had happened? A minute ago the leaves had been in a neat pile – now they were all over the place again!

He saw Tricky looking over the fence.

"Good-day, Dob," said Tricky politely. "It's a pity the wind blew your leaves away just as you got them into a pile, wasn't it?"

"The wind?" said Dob, puzzled. "But there isn't any wind."

"Well, it must have been a sudden, mischievous breeze, then," said Tricky, grinning. "You know – a little young wind that doesn't know any better."

"Hmm!" said Dob, and he swept up all his leaves into a pile again. It was dinner-time then, so he left them and went indoors. But he did

not get his dinner at once. He just watched behind his curtain to see if Tricky came into his garden to kick away his pile of leaves.

Well, he didn't see Tricky, of course, because that mischievous fellow had wriggled through the hole in the fence that was well hidden by the pile of leaves. He was now in the very middle of the pile – and to Dob's enormous surprise his leaves suddenly shot up in the air, and flew all over the grass.

"What a very peculiar thing!" said Dob, astonished. "I've never seen leaves behave like that before. Can it be that Tricky is right, and that a little breeze is playing about with them?"

He thought about it whilst he ate his dinner. It couldn't be Tricky, because Dob hadn't seen him climb over the fence and go to the pile. One minute the pile had been there, neat and tidy – and the next it had been scattered all over the place.

"I'll sweep up the leaves once more," thought Dob. "And I'll put them into my barrow before that wind gets them again."

But, of course, Tricky got into the next pile too, through the hole in the fence, and Dob found his leaves scattering all round him. He was very cross and very puzzled.

Soon Tricky called to him. He had wriggled out of the pile, through the hole in the fence and was now back in his own garden, grinning away at Dob. "My word – are you still sweeping up leaves? There's no end to it, Dob."

"I think you must have been right when you said that the wind is playing me tricks," said Dob. "But the thing is – what am I to do about it?"

"Catch the bad fellow and make him prisoner!" said Tricky.

"But how can you catch the wind?" asked Dob.

"Well, haven't you seen how the wind loves to billow out a sail, or blow out a sack or a balloon?" said Tricky. "Just get a sack, Dob, put the wind in it when it comes along, tie up the neck and send him off by carrier to the Weather Man to deal with. He'll give him a good spanking, you may be sure!"

"Well – if I *could* catch the wind that way I would certainly do all you say," said Dob. "But I'm afraid it isn't possible."

All the same he went and got a sack and put it ready nearby in case the wind did come along again. Tricky watched him sweep up his leaves once more, and he simply couldn't resist creeping through the hole to play the same trick on poor Dob again!

But this time Dob was on the watch for the wind, and as soon as he saw the leaves beginning to stir, he clapped the sack over the pile. He felt something wriggling in the leaves, and gave a shout.

"I've got him! I've caught the wind! He's filling up my sack! Aha, you scamp of a wind, I've got you!"

Tricky wriggled and shouted in the sack, but Dob shook him well down to the bottom of it, together with dozens of leaves, and tied up the neck firmly with rope.

"It's no good wriggling and shouting like that!" he said sternly. "You're caught. It's a good thing Tricky told me how to catch you! Now, off to the Weather Man you're going, and goodness knows what he'll do with you!" He wrote a big label:

"To be delivered to the Weather Man by the Carrier – one small, mischievous breeze. Suggest it should be well spanked before it is allowed to blow again."

And when the Carrier came by with his cart, Dob handed the whimpering Tricky to him, tightly tied up in the sack. The Carrier read the label and grinned.

"I'll deliver him all right," he said. "The Weather Man isn't in a very good temper lately – I'm afraid he'll spank this little breeze hard."

Dob went to look over the fence to find Tricky and tell him that his good idea had been carried out – but Tricky was nowhere to be seen, of course! And he was nowhere to be seen for three whole days! Dob was puzzled.

He came back the evening of the third day. He looked very solemn indeed. The Weather Man had spanked him well and truly, and had sent him to do all kinds of blowing jobs, which made Tricky very much out of breath.

"Hallo, Tricky! Wherever have you been?" cried Dob.

Tricky wouldn't tell him. He wouldn't tell anyone. But everyone agreed that his three days away had done him good – he wasn't nearly so mischievous, and ever since that day he has never played single trick on old Dob.

"I can't imagine why!" said Dob. How he would laugh if he knew!

The Bed That Took a Walk

THE pixie Miggle was always late for everything. If he went to catch a train he had to run all the way and then he would miss it. If he went to catch a bus it had always gone round the corner before he got there.

"It's just as easy to be early as to be late," said his friends. "Why don't you get up a bit sooner, then you would be in time for everything?"

"Well, I'm so sleepy in the mornings," said Miggle. "My wife comes and calls me, but I go off to sleep again. I really am a very tired person in the morning."

"Lazy, he means!" said his friends to one another. "Never in time for anything! It's shocking. One day he will be very sorry."

In the month of June the King and Queen of the pixies were coming to visit Apple Tree Town, where Miggle and his friends lived. The pixies were very excited.

"I shall get a new coat," said Jinky.

"I shall buy a new feather for my hat," said Twinkle.

"I shall have new red shoes," said Flitter.

"And I shall buy a whole new suit, a new hat and feathers, and new shoes and buckles with the money I have saved up," said Miggle. "I shall be very grand indeed!"

"You'll never be in time to see the King and Queen!" said Jinky, with a laugh.

"Indeed I shall," said Miggle. "I shall be up before any of you that day."

Well, the day before the King and Queen came, Miggle was very busy trying on his new things. The coat didn't quite fit, so he asked his wife to alter it. She stayed up very late trying to make it right.

It was about midnight when Miggle got to bed. How he yawned! "Wake me up at seven o'clock, wife," he said. "Don't forget."

Mrs. Miggle was tired. "I shall call you three times, and then, if you don't get up, I shan't call you any more," she said. "*I* have to call myself – nobody calls *me* – and I am tired tonight, so I shall not be very patient with you tomorrow if you don't get up when I call you."

"You *do* sound cross," said Miggle, and got into bed. He fell fast asleep, and it seemed no time at all before he felt Mrs. Miggle shouting in his ear, and shaking him.

"Miggle! It's seven o'clock. Miggle get up!"

"All right," said Miggle, and turned over to go to sleep again. In five minutes' time Mrs. Miggle shook him again, and once more he woke up, and went to sleep again.

"This is the third time I've called you," said Mrs. Miggle, ten minutes later, in a cross voice. "And it's the last time. If you don't get up now, I shan't call you any more."

"Right," said Miggle. "Just getting up, my dear." But he didn't. He went to sleep again. Plenty of time to get up and dress and go and see the King and Queen!

Mrs. Miggle kept her word. She didn't call Miggle again. She got dressed in her best frock and went to meet the King and Queen. Miggle slept on soundly, not hearing the footsteps going down the road, as all the pixies hurried by to meet the royal pair.

Miggle's bed creaked to wake him. It shook a little, but Miggle didn't stir. The bed was cross. It thought Miggle stayed too long in it. It knew how upset Miggle would be when he woke up and found that the King and Queen had gone.

So it thought it would take Miggle to the Town Hall, where the King and Queen would be, and perhaps he would wake up there.

The bed walked on its four legs to the door. It squeezed itself through, for it was a narrow bed. It trotted down the street, clickity-clack, clickity-clack.

Miggle didn't wake. He had a lovely dream that he was in a boat that went gently up and down on the sea, and said "clickity-clack" all the time.

"Gracious! Look, isn't that Miggle asleep on that bed?" cried Jinky, with a squeal of laughter. "The bed is wide awake, but Miggle isn't – so the bed is taking him to the Town Hall!"

"Clickity-clack, clickity-clack," went the four legs of the bed. Miggle gave a little snore. He was warm and cosy and comfy, and as fast asleep as ever.

The bed made its way into the Town Hall just as the King and Queen came on to the stage to speak to their people. The pixies jumped to their feet and cheered loudly.

The bed jumped up and down in joy, because it was enjoying the treat too. Miggle woke up when he heard the cheering, and felt the bumping of the bed. He sat up and looked round in the greatest surprise.

"Ha ha, ho ho, look at Miggle," shouted everyone, and the King and Queen had to smile too. Miggle was full of horror and shame! What happened! Had his silly bed brought him to the Town Hall? Oh dear, and he was in his pyjamas too, instead of in his lovely new clothes!

Miggle could have wept with shame. Mrs. Miggle saw him and went over to him.

"Really, Miggle! To think you've come to see the King and Queen in bed, not even dressed! I'm ashamed of you! What *can* you be thinking of?"

Miggle slid down into bed and pulled the clothes over his head. Mrs. Miggle pulled them off.

"Now you get up and bow properly to His Majesty the King and Her Majesty the Queen," she said.

"What, in my pyjamas?" said poor Miggle.

"Well, if you've come in pyjamas, you'll have to bow in them," said Mrs. Miggle. So Miggle had to stand up on the bed in his pyjamas and bow to the King and Queen. How they laughed!

"What a funny man!" said the Queen. "Does he often do things like this?"

Miggle didn't know what to do. He lay down again and ordered the bed to go home. But the bed wasn't a dog, to be ordered here and there. It wanted to stay and see the fun.

So Miggle had to jump out and run all the way home in his pyjamas. "How dreadful, how dreadful!" he kept thinking, as he ran. "I can't bear it! I'd better put on all my fine clothes, and go back and let the King and Queen see how grand I really am!"

So he did – but alas, when he got back to the Town Hall, the King and Queen had just gone. Everyone was coming away, pleased and excited. Miggle's bed trotted with them, "clickity-clack".

"Hallo, Miggle? Going to ride home asleep in bed?" cried his friends. "Oh, how you made the King and Queen laugh! It was the funniest sight we've ever seen."

Miggle frowned and didn't say a word. His bed tried to walk close to him, but he wouldn't let it. Horrid bed! "I'll never be late again!" thought Miggle. "Never, never, never!"

But he will. It's not so easy to get out of a bad habit. Won't it be funny if his bed walks off with him again?

He'll Do For a Sweep!

DICK was such a dirty little boy. His face was always grimy, he never washed his neck, or behind his ears, and as for his knees, well, you would think he walked on them, they were so dirty.

"I wish you didn't always look so dirty," said Miss Brown. "Don't you ever have a bath, Dick? Don't you ever wash your face? And look at your clothes! What have you been doing to them?"

Dick stared at his teacher. He didn't see why she should make such a fuss about dirt. What did it matter?

"It matters a lot," said Miss Brown. "A dirty person catches an illness more quickly than a clean one – and it looks so horrid to be dirty. It isn't polite to other people to go about looking so grimy and ugly."

Even then Dick didn't try to be clean. He never even cleaned his nails, and they looked really horrid.

"You look as if you've been sweeping

chimneys!" said Miss Brown, in disgust, one day when he came to school. "No, Dick – I really will not allow you to come to school in this state. You have soap and water at home, and I am sure you have some clean clothes somewhere. Go home, please, and come back clean."

Dick was cross. He walked out of school and went into the woods. He had to go through them to go home.

He hadn't gone very far before a little man rushed out of the trees and caught hold of him. "Here's one!" he cried, in excitement. "Here's one."

"Don't," said Dick, half-afraid. "Let me go."

Some other little men came running up. "Good!" they cried. "Come on – bring him along. Quick! Has he got any brushes?"

"He doesn seem to have," said the first little man. "Never mind – he can borrow mine."

"What do you mean? Where are you taking me?" yelled Dick, getting angry.

"We want you to sweep our chimney," said the first little man. "It's smoking terribly. Our own sweep has gone away, and we really must get the chimney done."

"But I'm not a sweep!" said Dick, crossly. "Can't you see I'm not?"

"You are! Sweeps are always grimy and dirty, they can't help it," said the little men. "You're grimy and dirty, so you must be a sweep. Come along!"

They dragged him along, though he didn't want to go. They came to a little cottage set in the heart of the wood. They took Dick inside. The fire was out, but it had been smoking very much, for the room was full of smoke, and Dick's eyes began to smart.

"Here are the brushes," said the little men, and they pushed a collection of poles and strange round brushes into Dick's hands. "Now sweep the chimney."

"I'm *not* a sweep!" wailed Dick.

"Well, you'll do for one. You can't get much dirtier than you are already," said the little men. "We will shut and lock the door, and we shan't let you out till you've swept our chimney for us!"

They locked the door and poor Dick was left in the smoky room. He stamped and raged. It was no good. The little men were not going to let him out till he had swept that chimney!

So he fitted the brush on top of a pole and

pushed it up the chimney. Then he fitted another pole to the end of that one and pushed it up still farther. Soot fell down in a cloud, and he coughed and choked. How dirty he got!

At last the brush stood out at the top of the chimney and all the soot was cleared. "Hurrah!" cried the little men, and opened the door. Poor Dick! You should have seen him. He was covered in soot from head to feet, and how he coughed and choked.

The little men let him go. "You aren't a real sweep, but you'll do for one, you're always so dirty," they said. "We will come and get you next time our chimney wants sweeping. We shall always know you, beause you are such a dirty boy."

Dick got into dreadful trouble when he went back home. His mother wouldn't believe that he had swept the chimney of all the little men. She thought he had got himself into more dirt than usual.

"No wonder Miss Brown sent you home!" she scolded. "Take off your clothes. Get into a hot bath. And keep yourself a bit cleaner in future, or I'll send you to bed each Saturday, and know that for one day at least you will have to keep clean."

Dick is much better now – not because he is afraid of being punished by his mother, but because he doesn't want those little men to use him for a sweep again. He's happier now he's cleaner – and he looks so much nicer!

The Spell That Didn't Stop

OLD Dame Quick-Eye put her head round the kitchen door, and lazy little Yawner jumped up at once.

"What! Reading again in the middle of the morning before you've done your work!" scolded Dame Quick-Eye. "Do you want me to put a spell on you and make you grow two more arms and hands? Then you'd have to do twice as much work!"

"Oh no, no," cried Yawner, shutting his book and beginning to bustle round at once. "Don't do that."

"I have three friends coming to dinner," said Dame Quick-Eye. "There are all the potatoes and apples to peel and the cabbage to cut up. I shall be very angry if everything isn't ready in time."

Yawner was very frightened when Dame Quick-Eye was angry. As soon as she had gone he rushed into the kitchen.

"The potatoes! The potatoes! Where are they? And what did I do with those cabbages?

Did I fetch them from the garden or didn't I? Where's the potato knife? Where is it?"

The potato knife was nowhere to be found. Yawner looked everywhere.

"Oh dear, oh dear – the only sharp knife I have! I can't peel the potatoes with a blunt one. I'll never have time to do all this peeling!"

The front door slammed. Yawner saw Dame Quick-Eye going down the path. He stopped rushing about and sat down. He yawned widely. "Oh dear, what am I to do? I'd better get a spell from the old Dame's room. A spell to peel potatoes and apples! She'll never know."

He tiptoed upstairs to the strange little room where Dame Quick-Eye did her magic and her spells. There they all were, in boxes and bottles on the shelf. "Spell for making things Big." "Spell for making things Small". "Spell for curing a Greedy Person". "Spell for growing more Arms and Hands". "Spell to cure Yawner of being Lazy".

"Oh dear," said Yawner, staring at the bottle with his name on the label. "I'd better not be lazy any more. Now – where's the spell to Peel Things Quickly?"

"Ah, here it is – good," he said at last, and picked up a box. In it was a green powder.

Yawner hurried downstairs and took up an ordinary knife. He rubbed a little of the green powder on the blade.

"Now peel!" he whispered. "Peel quickly, quickly. Don't stop!"

He rushed upstairs again and put the little box of powder back on the shelf. Then down he went. Dame Quick-Eye would never know he had taken a bit of her Peeling Spell.

The spell was already working. The knife was hovering over the bowl of potatoes in the sink, and one by one the potatoes rose up to be peeled, falling back with a plop. "A very pleasant sight to see," thought Yawner, and he bustled about getting ready the things he needed to lay the table.

The knife peeled all the potatoes in about two minutes. Then it started on the apples. Soon long green parings were scattered all over the draining-board and a dozen apples lay clean and white nearby.

Yawner shot a glance at the busy knife. "Splendid, splendid! Take a rest, dear knife."

He rushed into the dining-room to lay the lunch. He rushed back into the kitchen to get the plates – and how he stared! The potato knife was peeling the cold chicken that Yawner had put ready for lunch. It was scraping off long bits of chicken, which fell to the floor and were being eaten by a most surprised and delighted cat.

"Hey!" cried Yawner and rushed at the knife. "Stop that! You've done your work!"

He tried to catch the knife, but it flew to the dresser and peeled a long strip from that. Then it began to scrape the mantelpiece and big pieces of wood fell into the hearth.

Yawner began to feel frightened. What would Dame Quick-Eye say when she saw all this damage? He rushed at the knife again, but it flew up into the air, darted into the passage and disappeared.

"Well, good riddance to bad rubbish, I say," said Yawner loudly, and ran to put the potatoes on to boil. He heard Dame Quick-Eye come in with her friends and hurried even more. Lunch mustn't be late!

Then he heard such a to-do in the dining-room and rushed to see what the matter was. What a sight met his eyes!

The potato knife had peeled all the edges of the polished dining-room table. It had peeled every banana, orange, pear and apple in the dishes. It had peeled the backs of all the chairs, and even peeled the top off the clock.

"Look!" cried Dame Quick-Eye in a rage. "What's been happening? This knife is mad!"

"Bewitched, you mean," said one of her friends, looking at it closely. "I can see some green powder on the blade. Someone's been rubbing it with your Peeling Spell."

"It's that wretched tiresome lazy little Yawner then!" cried Dame Quick-Eye. "And there he is – peeping in at the door. Wait till I catch you!"

Yawner didn't wait to hear any more. He ran out into the garden. He kept his broomstick there, and he leapt on it at once.

"Off and away!" he shouted and up in the air rose the broomstick at once.

The broomstick soon became tired of going for miles and miles. It turned itself round and went home again. It sailed down to the yard. Yawner leapt off and rushed to the coal-cellar. He went in and slammed the door. Then he sank down on the coal and cried. Why had he been lazy? Why had he ever stolen a spell? Wrong deeds never, never did any good at all. Dame Quick-Eye looked in at the cellar window. She felt sorry for Yawner.

"Will you be lazy again?" she asked.

"No, Mam," wept Yawner.

"Will you ever steal my spells again?"

"No, Mam," said Yawner. "Never."

"Then come out and wash up the dirty plates and dishes," said Dame Quick-Eye, opening the door. "I've caught the knife and wiped the spell from it. You did a silly and dangerous thing."

"Yes, Mam," said Yawner mournfully, and went off to do the dishes.

Dame Quick-Eye hasn't had to use the special "Spell to cure Yawner of being Lazy". In fact, she has only to mention spells to make Yawner work twice as hard as usual.

It All Began With Jinky

ONCE upon a time Jinky the pixie looked over his garden wall into the garden next door.

"Dear me," said Jinky. "It does want digging up! I wonder why old Miss Tip-Tap doesn't get it done." So he asked her, and she told him.

"I've got a bad leg and I can't dig. I'm too poor to pay anyone. So I can't dig my garden and grow the lovely flowers that my bees like."

Jinky was kind. "We must help one another," he said. "I am strong. I will dig your garden for you, even though you cannot pay me."

So he dug Miss Tip-Tap's garden, and she planted flowers that made plenty of honey for her bees to collect. They buzzed in them all day long.

They put the honey in their hive and Miss Tip-Tap collected it and put it into jars. It was lovely honey, sweet and golden. It was a pity Jinky didn't like honey, or Miss Tip-Tap would have given him a jar or two.

"I'll give some to poor Dame Cough-a-Lot,"

she said. "She has such a bad throat. It will make it better."

So she went to Dame Cough-a-Lot and gave her three jars of the honey. It did Dame Cough-a-Lot's throat so much good that she was able to get up and go to wash and mend all Flitter-Wing's curtains and chair-covers.

"Oh, thank you!" said Flitter Wing. "Now I can have a party here for old Sir Dimity-Dot, who is staying with my aunt, and is feeling very dull since he had the flu."

So she gave a jolly party for Sir Dimity-Dot, and he was so pleased. He danced with Flitter-Wing, he ate four of her chocolate buns and had two slices of her iced cake, and he played hide-and-seek with everyone.

"Well!" he said, at the end of the party, "I don't know when I have enjoyed myself so much. Thank you, dear Flitter-Wing, thank you. You went to a lot of trouble for an old man, and I did enjoy it. Is there anything I can do for you? Or for your village? I should be very glad to, because I have enjoyed myself so much."

"Well," said Flitter-Wing, pleased, "could you see that we have a policeman of our very own? You see, we have to share Mr. Plod, who lives in the next village, and whenever we want him, he can't come. If we could have a policeman of our own, it would be lovely."

"Right," said Sir Dimity-Dot, who could do anything like that. "I'll send you a policeman the very next day."

So he did, and the policeman came along, looking very smart and clever. It was a good thing he came, too, because the next week Dame Treasure's jewels were stolen, and somebody was needed to catch the thief.

The policeman caught the thief, and put him into prison. But he didn't get back the jewels. So he wrote out a very big notice, and this is what it said:

Dame Treasure's jewels have been hidden by the thief, and he won't tell me where they are. A reward of one hundred pounds is offered to anyone who finds them.

Well, you can guess everyone hunted about for those jewels. Jinky hunted too, because he was very poor just then – so poor that he couldn't even buy jam to eat with his bread. It would be lovely, Jinky thought, to find the jewels and be rich for a change!

And suddenly Jinky found the jewels! He was trotting down Sandy Lane, when a rabbit popped his head out and spoke to him.

"Jinky! You once helped me when I hurt my paw. Now I'll help you. There's something in a bag down my hole that you might like to have. I've tried to eat what's inside, but it doesn't taste nice. Maybe you can cook it for your dinner."

Jinky bent down, and put his arm into the rabbit-hole. He pulled out a cloth-bag – and in it were all Dame Treasure's stolen jewels!

"Good gracious! I certainly shan't cook these!" said Jinky, in delight. "Why, they are jewels – and there is a reward offered for them too! Oh, Bobtail, what a darling you are. I shall take them straight to the policeman."

He did, and the policeman was glad. He gave Jinky the hundred pounds. "There you are," he said. "That's your reward. Spend it well."

"Oh, I shall!" said Jinky. "I shall put some in the bank. I shall buy myself a nice cake to eat and a pot of jam. I shall buy old Mother Shivers a warm black shawl. I shall—"

"Go along now and do a bit of spending then," said the policeman, and Jinky ran off in glee.

"Aren't I lucky, oh, aren't I lucky!" he sang as he went on. Miss Tip-Tap, who lived next door, heard him. She popped her head over the wall.

"No, you're not lucky!" she said. "You earned that money, Jinky – and I'll tell you how. Now you just listen to me, and see how your little bit of help to me went all the way round the village, and came back to you."

"Whatever do you mean?" said Jinky, surprised.

"Well, you dug up my garden for me, and I planted flowers for the bees. They made honey, and I gave some to old Dame Cough-a-Lot, and it made her throat so much better that she was able to go and wash curtains and covers for Flitter-Wing.

"And that meant that Flitter-Wing could give a party for old Sir Dimity-Dot, because then her house was nice and clean. And he was so pleased with the party, that he gave our village its new policeman.

"And when Dame Treasure's jewels were stolen, the new policeman caught the thief, and offered a reward for the jewels. And you found them, Jinky, and got the reward! So your little bit of help went all the way round and came back to you!"

"Oh, good!" cried Jinky. "I'll start it off again, shall I? I'll give a warm shawl to old Mother Shivers. Miss Tip-Tap, isn't it lovely to help one another!"

It is, isn't it? Let's think hard and see what we can do for somebody this very day!

Muddle's Mistake

THERE was once a brownie called Muddle. I expect you can guess why he had that name. He was always making muddles! He did make silly ones.

Once his mistress, the Princess of Toadstool Town, asked him to take a note to someone who lived in a fir tree. But Muddle came back saying that he couldn't find a tree with fur on at all!

Another time she asked him to get her a snapdragon – and he said he didn't mind fetching a dragon, but he didn't want to get one that snapped.

So, you see, he was always making muddles. And one day he made a very big muddle. The Princess always said he would.

"You just don't use your eyes, Muddle," she would say. "You go through the world without looking hard at things, without listening well with your ears, without using your brains. You are a real muddler!"

Now once the Princess was asked to a party

given by the Prince of Midnight Town. She was very excited.

"I shall go," she told Muddle. "You see, this prince gives really wonderful midnight parties, and he lights them by hanging glow-worms all over the place. It's really lovely!"

"Shall I go with you?" asked Muddle. "I expect you will need someone to look after you on your way to the party, because it will be dark."

"I think I shall fly there on a moth," said the Princess. "That will be nice. You get me a nice big moth, and you shall drive me."

"Very well, Your Highness," said Muddle, and he went off to get a moth. He hunted here and he hunted there, and at last he found a beautiful white-winged creature.

"Ah!" he said, "just the right moth for the Princess. I must get it to come with me. I will put it into a beautiful cage, and feed it on sugar and honey, so that it will stay with me until the night of the party."

So he spoke to the lovely creature. "Will you come home with me, White-Wings? I will give you sugar and honey. You shall stay with me until next week, when you may take the Princess of Toadstool Town to a party."

"I should like that," said White-Wings. "I love parties. Get on my back, brownie, and tell me which way to go to your home."

Muddle was pleased. He got on to White-Wings' back, and they rose high in the air. It was fun. They were soon at Muddle's house, which was a sturdy little toadstool, with a little green door in the stalk, and windows in the head.

"Shall I put you in a cage, or just tie you up, White-Wings?" asked Muddle. White-Wings didn't want to be put into a cage. So Muddle took a length of spider thread and tied her up to his toadstool. He brought her honey, and she put out her long tongue and sucked it up. Muddle watched her.

"What a wonderful tongue you have!" he said. "It is a bit like an elephant's trunk! I like the way you coil it up so neatly when you have finished your meal."

"It is long because I like to put it deep down into flowers, and suck up the hidden nectar," said White-Wings. "Sometimes the flowers hide their nectar so deep that only a very long tongue like mine can reach it."

Muddle told the Princess that he had found a very beautiful moth to take her to the midnight party. The Princess was pleased. "Well, I am glad you haven't made a muddle about *that*!" she said. "Bring White-Wings to me at twenty minutes to midnight and we will fly off. Make some reins of spider thread, and you shall drive."

Muddle was so pleased to be going to the party too. It was a great treat for him. He had a new blue suit made, with silver buttons, and a blue cap with a silver knob at the top. He looked very grand.

When the night came, Muddle went out to White-Wings. The lovely insect was fast asleep.

"Wake up," said Muddle. "It is time to go to the party."

White-Wings opened her eyes. She saw that it was quite dark. She shut her eyes again. "Don't be silly, Muddle," she said. "It is night-time. I am not going to fly in the dark."

"Whatever do you mean?" asked Muddle in surprise. "It is a midnight party! You *must* fly in the dark!"

"I never fly at night, never, never, never," said White-Wings. "Go away and let me sleep."

"But moths always fly at night!" cried Muddle. "I know a few fly in the day-time as well – but most of them fly at night. Come along, White-Wings. The Princess is waiting."

"Muddle, what is all this talk about moths?" asked White-Wings in surprise. "I am not a moth. I am a BUTTERFLY!"

Muddle lifted up his lantern and stared in the greatest surprise at White-Wings. "A b-b-b-butterfly!" he stammered. "Oh no – don't say that! No, no, say you are a moth!"

"Muddle, sometimes I think you are a very silly person," said the butterfly crossly. "Don't you know a butterfly from a moth? Have you lived all this time in the world, and seen hundreds of butterflies and moths, and never once noticed how different they are?"

"I thought you were a moth," said Muddle, and he began to cry, because he knew that the Princess would be very angry with him. "Please be a moth just for tonight and let me drive you to the midnight party."

"No," said White-Wings. "I am a butterfly and I don't fly at night. If I were you, I'd go and find a moth now, and see if you can get one that will take you."

"But how shall I know if I am talking to a moth or a butterfly?" said Muddle, still crying. "I might make a mistake again."

"Now listen," said the butterfly. "It is quite easy to tell which is which. Do you see the way I hold my wings? I put them neatly back to back, like this, so that I show only the underparts."

The white butterfly put her wings back to back. "Now," she said, "a moth never holds her wings like that. She puts them flat on her back – like this; or she wraps her body round with them – like this; or she just lets them droop – like this. But she certainly doesn't put them back to back."

"I'll remember that," said poor Muddle.

"Then," said the butterfly, "have a look at my body, will you, Muddle? Do you see how it is nipped in, in the middle? Well, you must have a look at the bodies of moths, and you will see that they are not nipped in, like mine. They are usually fat and thick."

"I will be sure to look," promised Muddle.

"And now here is a very important thing," said the butterfly, waving her two feelers under Muddle's nose. "A *most* important thing! Look at my feelers. What do you notice about them?"

"I see that they are thickened at the end," said Muddle. "They have a sort of knob there."

"Quite right," said White-Wings. "Now, Muddle, just remember this – a moth *never* has a knob or a club at the end of his feelers, never! He may have feelers that are feathery, or feelers that are just threads – but he will never have knobs on them like mine. You can always tell a butterfly or moth at once, by just looking at their feelers."

"Thank you, White-Wings," said Muddle, feeling very small. "All I knew was that butterflies flew in the day-time, and moths mostly flew at night. I didn't think of anything else."

"Now go off at once and see if you can find a moth to take you and the Princess to the party," said White-Wings. "I'm sleepy."

Well, off went poor Muddle. He looked here and he looked there. He came across a beautiful peacock butterfly, but he saw that it held its wings back to back as it rested, and that its feelers had thick ends. So he knew it wasn't a moth.

He found another white butterfly like White-Wings. He found a little blue butterfly, but its feelers had knobs on the end, so he knew that wasn't a moth, either.

Then he saw a pretty moth that shone yellow

in the light of his lantern. It spread its wings flat. Its feelers were like threads, and had no knob at the tips. It *must* be a moth. It left the leaf it was resting on and fluttered round Muddle's head.

"Are you a moth?" asked Muddle.

"Of course!" said the moth. "My name is Brimmy, and I am a brimstone moth. Do you want me?"

"Oh *yes*!" said Muddle. "Will you come with me at once, please, and let me drive you to the midnight party, with the Princess of Toadstool Town on your back?"

"Oh, I'd love that," said the moth, and flew off with Muddle at once. The Princess was cross because they were late, and Muddle did not like to tell her why.

They went to the party and they had a lovely time. Muddle set White-Wings free the next day, and gave her a little pot of honey to take away.

"You have taught me a lot," he said. "I shall use my eyes in future, White-Wings!"

Now let's have a game of Pretend! I am the Princess of Toadstool Town and you are just yourself. Please go out and see if you can find a moth to take me to a party! If you point out a butterfly to me instead, do you know what I shall call you?

I shall call you "Muddle" of course!

Dame Topple's Buns

IN Cherry Village there lived a small goblin called Pop. It was a funny name, but he was very greedy, you see, and his friends kept thinking he would one day eat too much, and go pop. They kept telling him this.

"You'll go pop! Why are you so greedy? It is disgusting. We shall call you Pop, because we are sure you will go pop!"

But even being called Pop didn't stop the little goblin from being greedy. Greedy people are always selfish, so Pop was not very much liked by the people of Cherry Village.

He always wanted the best of everything. He always wanted the biggest apple or the finest plum. He was quick too, so he could snatch or grab before anyone else could.

Now it is all very well to snatch and grab when you do it among people who can scold you, or can take back from you what you have grabbed. But it is very bad to do it to people who cannot stop you grabbing.

And that is what Pop began to do. He

stopped little Flitter the pixie in the street when he saw her carrying home a bag of sweets and he made her give him the very biggest. She had to because she was afraid of the fat little goblin.

Another day he helped old Mr. Limp across the road, and when Mr. Limp thanked him and said Pop could come into his garden and pick a few apples, what did Pop do but take his biggest basket and pick every apple off Mr. Limp's little tree!

That was greedy and unkind – but poor old Mr. Limp couldn't get them back because he couldn't run fast enough to catch the bad goblin.

"This sort of thing won't do," said the folk of Cherry Village, when they met in the street and talked about Pop's bad ways. "We must teach Pop a lesson. We must show him that it is not good to be greedy. He is getting more and more selfish, fatter and fatter, and horrider and horrider."

So they went to Dame Topple, who was a very clever old woman, and asked what to do with Pop.

She laughed. "I'll make some Balloon Buns," she said. "That will soon stop him from being greedy. You leave it to me."

"What are Balloon Buns?" said Jinky, in surprise.

"Well you can eat three with safety," said Dame Topple. "At the fourth you begin to swell up. At the fifth you almost burst your clothes. At the sixth you feel like a balloon. I don't know what happens at the seventh bun, because I have never seen people eat seven. I should think they would go pop."

"Can we all come to tea with you when you have made the Balloon Buns, and watch the fun?" asked Jinky, and Dame Topple said yes.

So the next Monday Pop and a good many of his friends were asked to tea at Dame Topple's. Pop was pleased about the invitation.

"She's a very good cook," he told the others. "She makes the finest cakes I know, and the loveliest pies. As for her buns and biscuits, well! I've never tasted anything like them. How I shall enjoy myself."

"Please don't be greedy," said Jinky. "I'm warning you, Pop. Please don't be greedy. You know we hate to see you taking the best of everything. It isn't nice. We don't like you when you are greedy."

"I don't care," said Pop, crossly. "I'm always hungry. And someone has got to have the biggest and best, so why not me, if I'm clever enough to get them?"

Nobody said any more. Pop had been warned. If he took no notice, it was his own fault.

You should have seen the table of goodies at Dame Topple's on that Monday afternoon! There was fruit salad and cream, all kinds of jellies, a great big chocolate cake, some ginger biscuits and, of course, the plate of Balloon Buns.

"Oooh," said Pop, taking a biscuit even before he sat down. "Ooooh! What a feast! Shall we begin?"

Well, of course, Pop had three times as much as anyone else. He took the biggest helping of everything, and he took the most cream, and more biscuits than anyone.

The Balloon Buns looked gorgeous. They were all different colours, just like small balloons. They shone strangely and they were scattered with sugar. Dame Topple said they were to be left till last.

Then everyone had three each – and oh, how delicious they were! "They taste of strawberries and pineapple and ice-cream and ginger-pop all mixed together!" said Jinky.

"There are four left," said Pop. He took one and ate it. He meant to finish them all up, he was so greedy. Everyone watched him.

He was fat, but when he had finished that fourth Balloon Bun he was much fatter! He took a fifth bun, and ate it quickly. How delicious it was!

Pop! A button flew off his coat. "You're bursting out of your clothes," said Jinky. "Be careful, Pop. Goodness, there goes another button – and look, the seam of your coat has burst all down your back!"

Pop took no notice. He was so afraid that someone else would eat the last two buns that he put them both on to his own plate. He ate the sixth one, and then he looked round at everyone.

"I feel a bit funny," he said. "Rather like a balloon. I feel sort of light and poppish."

"You'll go pop," said Jinky, alarmed. "Oh, don't eat any more!"

But Pop was not going to miss that last Balloon Bun. He put it into his mouth and chewed it. And then a most peculiar thing happened. He floated up into the air! He went up like a little balloon and there he floated, bumping his head against the ceiling.

"What's happened?" he shouted in alarm. "Get me down, quick!" But as soon as someone pulled him down by his fat legs, he floated up again.

"You really would go pop now if anyone stuck a pin in you!" said Jinky. "You are just like a balloon. Whatever will happen to you?"

Well, they all got him down to the ground, and tried to take him home. But as soon as he got out of doors, up he went into the air again, and floated out of sight!

"He's gone," said Jinky. "Poor old Pop. He's gone above the clouds, out of sight. What an awful punishment for being greedy."

"If he falls into a holly-bush, he really will go pop now," said Dame Topple. "Well, well – Balloon Buns for Greedy People ought to be sold all over the country. I think I'll do that –it will soon stop greediness, I'm sure!"

She's right, too! I don't expect you're greedy, but if you are, don't eat more than three Balloon Buns, will you? You might go and join poor Pop, wherever he is, if you do!

The Train That Went to Fairyland

ONCE, when Fred was playing with his railway train in the garden, a very strange thing happened.

Fred had just wound up his engine, fastened the carriages to it, and sent them off on the lines, when he heard a small, high voice.

"That's it, look! That's what I was telling you about!"

Fred looked round in surprise. At first he saw no one, then, standing by a daisy, he saw a tiny fellow dressed in a railway guard's uniform, but he had little wings poking out from the back of his coat! He was talking to another tiny fellow, who was dressed like a porter. They were neither of them any taller than the nearest daisy.

"Hallo!" said Fred, in surprise. "Who are you and what do you want?"

"Listen," said the tiny guard. "Will you lend us your train just for a little while, to go to Goblin Town and back? You see, the chief goblin is taking a train from Toadstool Town and our engine has broken down. We can't get enough magic in time to mend it – the chief goblin is getting awfully angry."

"Lend you my train?" said Fred, in the greatest astonishment and delight. "Of course I will, but you must promise me something first."

"What?" asked the little guard.

"You must make me small and let *me* drive the train," said Fred.

"All right," said the guard. "But you won't have an accident, will you?"

"Of course, not," said Fred. "I know how to drive my own train!"

"Shut your eyes and keep still a minute," said the guard. Fred did as he was told, and the little guard sang out a string of very strange words. And when Fred opened his eyes again, what a surprise for him! He was as small as the tiny guard and porter.

"This is fun!" said Fred, getting into the cab. "Come on. Will the engine run all right without lines, do you suppose?"

"Oh, we've got enough magic to make those as we go along," said the little guard, and at once some lines spread before them, running right down the garden to the hedge at the bottom. It was very strange and exciting.

"Well, off we go!" said Fred. "I suppose the engine has only got to follow the lines, and it will be all right!"

He pulled down the little handle that started the train, and off they went! The guard and the porter had climbed into the cab of the engine too, so it seemed rather crowded. But nobody minded that, of course.

The lines spread before them in a most magical manner as the train ran over them, down the garden, through a hole in the hedge,

and then goodness me, down a dark rabbit-hole!

"Hallo, hallo!" said Fred in surprise. "Wherever are we going?"

"It's all right," said the little guard. "This will take us to Toadstool Town. We come up at the other side of the hill."

The engine ran through the winding rabbit-holes, and once or twice met a rabbit who looked very scared indeed. Then it came up into the open air again, and there was Toadstool Town!

"I should have known it was without being told," said Fred, who looked round him in delight as they passed tiny houses made out of the toadstools growing everywhere. "Hallo, we're running into a station!"

So they were. It was Toadstool Station. Standing on another line was the train belonging to the little guard. The engine-driver and stoker were trying their hardest to rub enough magic into the wheels to start it, but it just wouldn't go!"

On the platform was a fat, important-looking goblin, stamping up and down.

"Never heard of such a thing!" he kept saying, in a loud and angry voice. "Never in my life! Keeping me waiting like this! Another minute and I'll turn the train into a caterpillar, and the driver and stoker into two leaves for it to feed on!"

"What a horrid fellow!" whispered Fred. The guard ran to the goblin and bowed low.

"Please, your Highness, we've got another train to take you home. Will you get in?"

"About time something was done!" said the goblin, crossly. "I never heard of such a thing in my life, keeping me waiting like this!"

He got into one of the carriages. He had to get in through the roof, because the doors were only pretend ones that wouldn't open. The little guard slid the roof open and then shut it again over the angry goblin.

"Start up the train again quickly!" he cried. So Fred pulled down the handle again and the little clockwork train set off to Goblin Town. It passed through many little stations with strange names, and the little folk waiting there stared in the greatest surprise to see such an unusual train.

Fred was as proud and pleased as could be! He drove that engine as if he had driven engines all his life. He wished and wished he could make it whistle. But it only had a pretend whistle. Fred wished the funnel would smoke, too, but of course, it didn't!

Suddenly the train slowed down and stopped. "Good gracious! What's the matter?" said the little guard, who was still in the engine-cab with Fred. "Don't say your train is going to break down, too? The goblin certainly *will* turn us all into something unpleasant if it does!"

The goblin saw that the train had stopped. He slid back the roof of his carriage and popped his angry face out.

"What's the matter? Has this train broken down, too?"

Fred had jumped down from the cab and had gone to turn the key that wound up the engine. It had run down, and no wonder, for it had come a long, long way! It was surprising that it hadn't needed winding up before.

The goblin stared in astonishment at the key in Fred's hand. He had never seen a key to wind up an engine before. He got crosser than ever.

"What are you getting down from the engine for? Surely you are not going to pick flowers or do a bit of shopping? Get back at once!"

But Fred had had enough of the cross goblin. He tapped him hard on the head with the key, and slid the roof back so that the goblin couldn't open it again.

"Now you be quiet," said Fred. "The pixies and elves may be frightened of you, but *I'm* not! Here I've come along with my train to help you and all you do is to yell at me and be most impolite. I don't like you. I'll take you to Goblin Town with pleasure, and leave you there with even greater pleasure, but while we are on the way you will please keep quiet and behave."

Well! The little guard and porter nearly fell out of the cab with horror and astonishment when they heard Fred speaking like that to the chief goblin! But Fred only grinned, and wound up the engine quickly.

There wasn't a sound from the goblin. Not a sound. He wasn't used to being spoken to like that. He thought Fred must be a great and mighty wizard to dare to speak so angrily to him. He was frightened. He sat in his roofed-in carriage and didn't say a word.

The train went on to Goblin Town and stopped. Fred got down, slid back the roof of the goblin's carriage and told him to get out.

The goblin climbed out quickly, looking quite scared.

"What do you say for being brought here in my train?" said Fred, catching hold of the goblin's arm tightly.

"Oh, th-th-thank you," stammered the goblin.

"I should think so!" said Fred. "I never heard of such a thing, not thanking anyone for a kindness. You go home and learn some manners, goblin."

"Yes, yes, I will, thank you, sir," said the chief goblin, and ran away as fast as ever he could. Everyone at the station stared in amazement.

"However did you dare to talk to him like that?" said the little guard in surprise. "Do you know, that is the first time in his life he has ever said, 'Thank you'! What a wonderful boy you are!"

"Not at all," said Fred, getting back into the engine-cab. "That's the only way to talk to rude people. Didn't you know? Now then, back home we go, to my own garden!"

And back home they went, past all the funny little stations to Toadstool Town, down into the rabbit-burrows and out into the field, through the hedge and up the garden, back to where they started.

"Shut your eyes and we'll make you your own size again," said the little guard. In a trice Fred was very large indeed and his train now looked very small to him!

"What would you like for a reward?" said the little guard. "Shall I give your train a real whistle, and a real smoke in its tunnel? Would you like that?"

"Rather!" said Fred. And from that very day his clockwork engine could whistle and smoke exactly like a real one.

Little Mister Sly

MISTER Sly lived in a small cottage at the edge of Lilac Village. He kept hens and sold the eggs, but he never gave any away. He was a mean little man, and was only generous when he thought he would get something out of it.

Now one day Sly found six eggs that one of his hens had laid away from the hen-house. He felt sure they had been laid weeks ago, because for at least seven weeks he had shut up his hens carefully, and not let them stray.

"What a pity! They will be bad!" he said to himself. "All wasted!"

Then he thought hard. "I could give them away. I'll give them to old Mister Little-Nose. He can't smell anything bad or good since he had the flu last year. Maybe he will give me some honey from his bees then."

So Sly put the eggs into a round basket and took them to Mister Little-Nose.

"Oh, thank you!" said Mister Little-Nose. "That's kind of you, Sly. I will give you some honey in the summer-time."

After Sly had gone, Mister Little-Nose heard someone knocking at his door again, and dear me, it was the carrier, bringing twelve eggs for him from his sister.

"Well, well – I've too many eggs now," he thought. "I'll send some to the pixie Twinkle."

So he sent his little servant round to Twinkle with the six eggs that Sly had given him. But before Twinkle could use them she had to leave in a hurry to go and see her aunt, who was ill.

"I'll take the eggs to old Dame Groan," she thought. "She's been ill and needs feeding up."

So she took them to Dame Groan's house and left them outside the door, because Dame Groan was asleep. Twinkle could hear her snoring.

Dame Groan grumbled when she saw the eggs. "Twinkle might have known that the doctor has said eggs are the one thing I mustn't eat!" she said. "What a pity! Well, Twinkle is away, so I can't give them back to her. I'll give them to old Miss Scared. She can do with a bit of good luck, she's so poor."

Miss Scared was simply delighted with them. "Oh, thank you, dear Dame Groan," she said. "I do hope you are feeling better now. Thank you very much."

But before Miss Scared could eat any of the eggs, there came another knock at her door. She opened it. Outside stood Mister Sly, a horrid mean look on his face.

"I lent you fifty pence last week," he said. "And you said you would pay me sixty pence back this week. Where is the money?"

"Oh, Mister Sly, I haven't got it. Won't you wait till tomorrow?" said Miss Scared. "Please do."

"Can't wait," said Mister Sly. Then he caught sight of the six eggs. "Hullo – you've got six eggs! Give me these six eggs, and I'll let you off."

"All right," said poor Miss Scared with a sigh, for she had badly wanted an egg for her tea. "Take them."

Mister Sly went off with the eggs. He didn't know they were the very same old eggs he had taken to Mister Little-Nose that very morning.

"I'll have bacon and eggs for tea," he said, and got out his pan. He put in his bacon and it sizzled well. He put in a few mushrooms – and then he cracked an egg on the side of the pan, and let it run in, among the bacon and mushrooms.

But oh dear, it was bad! Mister Sly managed

to scrape it out, and tried another egg. That was
bad too. They were all bad! The worst of it was
that his bacon tasted of bad egg when he ate it,
and the whole kitchen smelt dreadful. Mister
Sly felt very sick.

He was very, very angry. "That dreadful
Miss Scared!" he said. "How dare she give me
bad eggs! This is a matter for the police. I will
call Mr. Plod in and tell him all about it. He
will give Miss Scared a good talking-to, and
that will scare her properly."

So he went to Mr. Plod and told him. Then

he and Mr. Plod went to Miss Scared's cottage, and he knocked on the door.

"You bad woman! You gave me rotten eggs!" said Sly, angrily. "Where did you get them from?"

"Oh, Dame Groan sent them to me," said Miss Scared, as frightened as could be. "Please, please, don't blame me. I didn't know they were bad. I really didn't."

"Ha – Dame Groan," said Mr. Plod, and wrote the name in his notebook. "Come along – we'll go and see her."

So they went to Dame Groan. "Those eggs you gave Miss Scared were bad!" scolded Sly. "How dare you give away rotten eggs?"

"I didn't know they were bad," said Dame Groan, in a rage, "and don't you talk to me like that, Sly. Twinkle sent me those eggs – she said that Mister Little-Nose had given them to her."

"We'll go to Mister Little-Nose then," said Mr. Plod. "Ah – there he is, just over there! Hi, Little-Nose, I've got something to ask you."

"What?" said Little-Nose.

"Well, Sly here is trying to trace a batch of bad eggs he had given to him," said Mr. Plod. "It seems that Miss Scared gave them to him, and Dame Groan gave them to her, and Twinkle gave them to Dame Groan, and you gave them to Twinkle. Now – did your hens lay them? And what right have you to send out bad eggs?"

"I've got no hens," said Mister Little-Nose, in surprise. "and as for who gave them to me – well, Sly should know, for he sent them round himself!"

"What!" cried Mr. Plod, and snapped his notebook angrily. "What! Did you give him six bad eggs, Sly? And you have dared to come and complain to me about them and waste my time, when they were your eggs! You must have known they were bad, too. How dare you, I say?"

Sly hadn't a word to say for himself. Little-Nose looked at him in disgust.

"He always was mean," he said. "He'd never give away anything good. I might have guessed they were bad. Well, I'm glad they came back to you, Sly, very glad. Serves you right!"

And so it did.

The Brownie's Magic

ONE night the snow came. It fell quietly all night through, and in the morning, what a surprise for everyone! The hills were covered with snow. The trees were white. The bushes were hidden, and the whole world looked strange and magical.

Bobbo the brownie looked out of his cave in the hillside. The path down to the little village was hidden now. The path that ran over the top of the hill had gone too.

"Snow everywhere," said Bobbo. "Beautiful white snow! How I love it! I wish I had watched it falling last night, like big white goose feathers."

He saw someone coming up the hill, and he waved to him.

"Ah!" he said, "there is my clever cousin, Brownie Bright-Eyes. I wonder what he has brought to show me today. He is always bringing me wonderful things."

Brownie Bright-Eyes walked up the hill in the snow, making deep footprints as he came, for he carried something large and heavy.

"What have you got there?" said Bobbo, when Bright-Eyes at last came to his cave. "You are always bringing me something strange and wonderful to see, Bright-Eyes."

"I have made a marvellous mirror," panted Bright-Eyes, bringing the shining glass into the cave. "I do think I am clever, Bobbo. I made this magic mirror myself. I think I must be the cleverest brownie in the world."

"Don't boast," said Bobbo. "I don't like you when you boost."

"I am not boasting!" cried Bright-Eyes crossly. "Wait till you do something clever yourself, and then scold me for boasting. It's a pity you don't use your own brains."

"I do," said Bobbo. "But you are always so full of your own wonderful doings that you never listen to me when *I* want to tell you something."

"I don't expect you would have anything half so wonderful to tell me as I have to tell you," said Bright-Eyes. "Now – just look at this mirror."

Bobbo looked at it. It was a strange mirror, because it didn't reflect what was in front of it. It was just dark, with a kind of mist moving in the glass. Bobbo could see that it was very magic.

"I can't see anything," said Bobbo.

"No, you can't – but if you want to know where anyone is – Tippy the brownie for instance – the mirror will show you!"

"What do you mean?" asked Bobbo, astonished.

"Now look," said Bright-Eyes. He stroked the shining mirror softly. "Mirror, mirror, show me where Tippy the brownie is!"

And at once a strange thing happened. The mist in the glass slowly cleared away – and there was Tippy the brownie, sitting in a bus. The mirror showed him quite clearly.

"Isn't that wonderful?" said Bright-Eyes. "You couldn't possibly have told me where Tippy was, without the help of the mirror, could you?"

"Yes, I could," said Bobbo. "I knew he was in the bus."

"You didn't!" said Bright-Eyes.

"I did," said Bobbo.

"Then you must have seen Tippy this morning," said Bright-Eyes.

"I haven't," said Bobbo. "*You* found out where he was by using your magic mirror, but

I, Bright-Eyes, *I* found out by using my brains! So I am cleverer than you."

Bright-Eyes didn't like that. He always wanted to be the cleverest person anywhere. He frowned at Bobbo.

"I expect it was just a guess on your part that Tippy was in the bus," he said. "Now – can you tell me where Jinky is – you know, the pixie who lives down the hill?"

"Yes," said Bobbo at once. "He's gone up the hill to see his aunt, who lives over the top."

Bright-Eyes rubbed the mirror softly. "Mirror, mirror, show me where Jinky is!" he said. And at once the mirror showed him a pixie, sitting in a chair, talking to a plump old lady. It was Jinky, talking to his aunt!

"There you are, you see – I was right," said Bobbo, pleased. "I am cleverer than your mirror. It uses magic – but I use my brains. I can tell you a lot of things that *you* could only get to know through your magic mirror – but which *I* know by using my very good brains. Ha, ha!"

"What can you tell me?" asked Bright-Eyes.

"I can tell you that Red-Coat the fox passed by here in the night, although I did not see or hear him," said Bobbo. "I can tell you that six rabbits played in the snow down the hill this morning. I can tell you that Mother Jane's ducks left the frozen pond today and went to her garden to be fed."

"You must have seen them all. That's easy," said Bright-Eyes.

"I tell you, I have not seen anything or anyone today except you," said Bobbo. "I know all this by using my brains."

"What else do you know?" asked Bright-Eyes, thinking that Bobbo must really be cleverer than he thought.

"I know that the sparrows flew down to peck crumbs that Mother Jane scattered for them," said Bobbo. "I know that Crek-Crek the moorhen took a walk by the side of the pond. I know that Mother Jane's cat ran away from Tippy's dog this morning. And I know that Tippy's cow wandered from its shed, and then went back to it."

Bright-Eyes stared at Bobbo in wonder. "You are very clever to know all this, if you did not see anyone," he said. "I shall ask my magic mirror if what you say is true!"

He stroked the glass and asked it many things – and each time the glass showed him that what Bobbo said was true! There was the cat chasing the dog. There was the moorhen walking over the snow. There was Tippy's cow wondering all about!

"Please tell me your magic," said Bright-Eyes to Bobbo. "It must be very good magic to tell you all these things."

"Well – come outside and I will show you how I know them all," said Bobbo, beginning to laugh. They went outside, and Bobbo pointed to the crisp white snow. There were many marks and prints in it, as clear as could be.

"Look," said Bobbo, pointing to some small footprints that showed little pointed toes. "Tippy always wears pointed shoes – and do you see how deep his footprints are? That shows that he was running. Why was he running? To catch the bus! That's how I knew where he was, without having seen him."

"How did you know about Jinky going to see his aunt?" asked Bright-Eyes.

Bobbo pointed to some very big footprints. "Those are Jinky's marks," he said. "He has enormous feet. The footprints are going up the hill, and the only person Jinky goes to see over the top is his aunt. So I knew where Jinky was!"

"Very clever," said Bright Eyes.

"And I knew that Red-Coat the fox had

passed in the night because there are *his* footprints," said Bobbo, pointing to a set of rather dog-like marks that showed the print of claws very clearly. "I knew it was Red-Coat because I saw the mark his tail made here and there behind his hind feet – see it?"

Bright-Eyes saw the mark of the fox's tail in the snow, and the line of footprints too.

Bobbo took Bright-Eyes farther down the hill. He showed him the rabbit-prints – little marks for the front feet and longer, bigger ones for the strong hind feet. He showed him where Mother Jane's ducks had walked from the pond to her garden.

"You can see they were ducks because they have left behind them the mark of their webbed feet," he said. "And you can see where the sparrows fed because they have left little prints in pairs – they hop, you see, they don't walk or run – so their prints are always in pairs."

"And there are the moorhen's marks," said Bright-Eyes. "He has big feet rather like the old hen at home, although he is a waterbird. But he runs on land as well as swims on water, so he doesn't have webbed feet. Look how he puts them one in front of the other, Bobbo, so the footprints are in a straight line!"

"And there are the marks made by Tippy's cow," said Bobbo. "You can tell each hoof-mark quite well. And Mother Jane's cat ran *here* – look at the neat little marks. And Tippy's dog ran *here* – you can tell the difference, because the cat puts her claws *in* when she runs, so they don't show in her footprints, but the dog doesn't – so his *do* show!"

"Bobbo, you are very, very clever," said Bright-Eyes. "You are cleverer than I am. It is better to use your eyes and your brains, than to use a magic mirror! I think you are the cleverest brownie in the world!"

Would you like to be as clever as Bobbo? Well, go out into the snow, when it comes, and read the footprints you find there! You will soon know quite a lot.

Little Connie Careless

THERE was once a little girl whose name was Connie. Everyone called her Connie Careless, and you can guess why.

Oh, she was careless! She lost something nearly every day. She lost her hankies, she lost her hats, she lost her books, she even lost her dear little watch that her father gave her for Christmas.

"It's no good giving Connie anything," said her mother. "She never takes care of a thing. She's so careless. I do wish I could cure her."

But Connie didn't try to be cured. She didn't try to remember where she had put anything, she didn't try to think at all.

"I've lost my gloves!" she would wail. "I don't know where I put them! I must have left them in the bus.

"I've lost my pencil, and it was a new one! I've lost the ten pence Daddy gave me, and I wanted to buy some sweets. I've lost my ruler too."

The things Connie lost! She once lost her

lovely teddy bear. She lost the clockwork clown that her aunt gave her, and she even lost a box of skittles, though how she did that she couldn't think! You see, she had been carrying them home when her shoe came undone. She had put the box of skittles on a wall, whilst she did up her shoe – and when she stood up again, she forgot about the skittles and went home!

"It's no good lending Connie a book, she will never remember to give it back," said Bob.

"It's no good lending her anything," said Lily. "She always loses everything."

"She's lost her umbrella again," said Ronnie. "That's the fourth one she's lost."

"And last week she lost her mackintosh," said Margery. "I should think her mother must get very cross with her."

Her daddy was very cross too. "What is the good of my working hard and earning money to spend on nice things for you, if you don't care enough for them to keep them?" he said, angrily. "I wanted to buy myself some new books this week, and now I must use that money to buy you another mackintosh to replace the one you lost. You are a bad, careless unkind little girl."

Connie went into the garden and cried. She

hadn't thought before that her carelessness might rob her daddy of something he badly wanted himself.

"I wish I had a cure for the way I lose things," she wept. "I wish I had."

"I can give you one," said a little voice, and a small green imp popped his head up from behind a pansy. Connie stared at him. She didn't know that imps played tricks, and should never be trusted.

"I wish you would give me a cure," she said. "Please do."

"Eat this," said the imp and threw her something that looked like a small sweet. "Eat it, and say, 'I wish all the things I ever lost would come back again. I wish I was cured of being careless!'"

Connie ate the sweet, and the imp popped down behind the pansy. Nothing happened. Connie was disappointed. Then her mother called her and sent her down to the shops for something.

Now, as she came back, Connie heard a funny pattering noise behind her, and she turned to see what it was – and what do you think she saw?

All the things she had ever lost were coming after her! There were hundreds and hundreds of them in a long, long line. There were gloves and hats, hankies and shoes, her mackintosh, four little umbrellas, a coat, all kinds of money, books and papers, the skittles all jumping along out of their box, the big teddy bear carrying her watch in one hand, the clockwork clown and a rabbit.

Connie was frightened. She turned and ran, and everything tore after her. She couldn't get rid of them. They galloped along, the teddy bear now at the very front.

"Stop!" he cried. "We belong to you! Stop!"

But Connie wouldn't stop. Everyone stared and how they laughed!

"Look at all that Connie has lost in her seven years!" they said. "What a careless child!"

She rushed in at her garden gate and slammed it. The teddy bear couldn't open it. The little green imp popped his head up and grinned.

"Shall I let them in?" he said. "They belong to you. Don't you like my magic?"

"No, I don't, it frightens me," wept Connie. "Make them go away. I never saw so many things in my life. I don't like them. I'll never, never lose anything else if only you'll make them go away!"

"Ping!" said the imp, making a noise like a bell – and at once all the lost things vanished! Where they went to, Connie didn't know. She only knew that they were gone. She hurried indoors, sobbing.

"What's the matter?" said Mummy, and Connie told her the whole story. Mummy really couldn't believe it, so Connie took her out into the garden to show her the green imp behind the pansy plant.

But he wasn't there. Mummy shook her head. "You've been imagining it all," she said. "If it was really true, Connie, I know you would be careful in future, and would never lose anything else!"

"Well, I never shall!" said Connie. "So you'll know it's all true!"

It's a very funny thing, but Connie has never lost anything since, and now we call her Connie Careful instead of Connie Careless. Nobody has ever seen that green imp again, but he certainly managed to cure Connie, didn't he?

The Three Bad Imps

THERE were once three bad imps. They were called Snip, Snap and Snorum, and they really were very naughty. They were very small – not even as tall as a daisy. They had all kinds of jobs to do, and they did them very badly.

They were supposed to help the moths when they crept out of their cocoons – but they pulled them out so roughly that sometimes they spoilt the wings of the little creatures. They had to polish the little coppery beetles that ran through the grasses – and sometimes they polished the beetles' feet too, so that they slipped and slid all over the place!

They were always up to naughty tricks, and nobody could ever catch them to punish them. They were so small, and could hide so easily.

"Nobody will ever catch *me*!" Snip would boast, as he swung up and down on a grass-blade.

"And I can always hide where nobody can find me!" said Snap.

"We're as clever as can be!" said Snorum.

And so they were. They got into trouble every day, but they slipped out of it as easily as worms slip out of their holes!

But one day they really went too far. They had been told to brush the hairs of a furry caterpillar who had fallen into the mud and got very dirty. And instead of brushing his hairs and making him nice and clean again, Snip, Snap and Snorum cut off all his hairs to make themselves little fur coats!

Well, of course, the caterpillar complained very loudly indeed, and the pixies set off to find and catch the three bad imps.

"We'll punish them well!" said the biggest pixie. "I shall spank each of them with a good, strong grass-blade!"

But nobody could catch those naughty imps. They hid here, and they hid there – and even when they were found, they slipped away easily.

"They have polished themselves all over with the polish they use for the beetles," said the biggest pixie. "So, even if we get hold of them, we can't hold them! They slip out of our hands like eels."

"What shall we do, then?" asked the smallest pixie. "How can we catch them?"

"Well, first we must find them," said the biggest pixie. "Now – where can they be?"

"Send the ants to find out," said another pixie. "They can run here, there and everywhere, and they will soon find where they are hiding."

So the little brown ants were sent hurrying through the wood, between the grasses, to find the hidden imps. One ant found them and came hurrying back.

"They are asleep in the leaves of the honeysuckle, where it climbs high," said the tiny ant. "If you come now, you could catch them."

"They will slip out of our hands as soon as we touch them," said the pixies. "If only we could trap them. Little ant, where could we find a trap that will hold the imps?"

"Only the spiders make traps," said the ant. "You might ask *them*."

So the pixies called the spiders, and they came running over the grass on their eight legs, their eyes looking wisely at the pixies.

"Come with us," said the pixies. "We want you to make a trap for some naughty imps."

So, all together, the pixies and the spiders ran to the honeysuckle, where it climbed high. Softly they all climbed up the twisted stems, and came to where the imps were lying fast asleep among the honeysuckle leaves.

"Can you make a trap to catch them?" whispered the pixies. The spiders looked at one another. Yes – they could!

"There are six of us," said a fine big spider. "We can make a cage, if you like – a six-sided cage of web, that will hold the three naughty imps as long as you like!"

"Oh *yes*!" cried the pixies. "Make six webs, in the form of a square – four for the sides, one for the top and one for the bottom. That will be a splendid cage. But be careful not to wake the imps."

The spiders began their work. The pixies watched them. The spiders were very clever indeed. Underneath each spider were little lumps, and from them they drew the thread for their webs.

"These are our spinnerets," said a big spider to a pixie. "We spin our web from them. The thread isn't really made till it oozes out of our spinnerets, you know. It squeezes out like a liquid, and the air makes it set, so that we get threads to work with."

"It's like magic," said the pixies in wonder. They watched the spiders pull the thread from their spinnerets, more and more and more – as much as they needed.

"Feel the thread," said a spider. "It's so fine – and yet so strong."

"Yes, it is," said the pixies. "We would like some to sew our party frocks with! Hurry, spiders, or the imps will wake."

Each spider chose a leaf, stalk or twig to hang her outer threads on. It was marvellous to watch them.

After they had fixed their outer threads, they began to make threads that ran to the middle and back, like spokes of a wheel. The three imps slept soundly all the time, for the spiders made no noise at all.

"See how the spiders use their clawed feet to guide the thread," whispered a pixie. The pixies watched in delight. "Oh look – now the spiders are running a spiral thread round and round the spokes!"

So they were. They had finished all the spokes, and were now moving round their webs, letting out a thread that went round and round in smaller and smaller circles.

"The imps will never, never be able to escape from this trap," said a pixie.

"We will make the web sticky too," said a

spider. "If we hang tiny sticky drops along the threads, the imps will find themselves caught fast if they try to break through!

"I have seen flies caught in webs," said pixies. "I suppose the stickiness holds them fast, spider?"

"Of course," said the spider, pulling a thread tighter. "Now – we have finished. Shall we go and hide under leaves, and watch what happens?"

"Yes," said the pixies. So the spiders ran up to some leaves, and hid themselves there, waiting silently, just as they did when they waited for flies to come.

Soon the imps awoke and stretched themselves – and they saw the trap they were in! They jumped to their feet in alarm.

"What's this! We're in a cage!"

"It's a cage made of spider's web!"

"Break it, break it!"

The three imps flung themselves against the webby walls of the strange cage. They broke the threads – but in a trice the sticky web fell on their arms and legs and heads – and they were caught!

They struggled, and they wriggled, but it was no use. The strong, sticky threads held them as tightly as they could hold flies. Down rushed the spiders and, pouring out more thread from their spinnerets, they rolled the imps round and round in it, until they were helpless.

"Thank you, spiders," said the pixies. "We are very grateful to you. Now at last we have caught these bad little imps! They will be well punished!"

"If you want our help again at any time, just let us know," said the spiders. "We'll come running to you on our eight long legs!"

The imps were carried off by the pixies – and dear me, didn't they get well spanked! They sobbed and they cried, and they promised they would be as good as gold.

And so far, they have – you'll find that the caterpillars have their hairs well brushed, and the ladybirds and beetles are well polished now.

But the imps keep away from the spiders. They have never forgotten how they were caught in a webby trap, spun by the six clever spiders!

Silky and The Snail

SILKY was a pixie. She lived under a hawthorn hedge, and often talked to the birds and animals that passed by her house.

One day a big snail came crawling slowly by. Silky had never seen a snail, and at first she was quite afraid. Then she ran up to the snail, and touched his hard shell.

"How clever you are!" she said. "You carry your house about with you! Why do you do that?"

"Well, you see," said the snail, "I have a very soft body that many birds and other creatures like to eat – so I grow a shell to protect it."

"What a good idea," said the pixie. "Can you put your body right inside your shell, snail?"

"Watch me!" said the snail, and he curled his soft body up quickly into his shell. There was nothing of him to be seen except his spiral shell.

"Very clever," said the pixie. "Come out again, please, snail. I want to talk to you."

The snail put his head out and then more of his body. He had four feelers on his head, and the pixie looked at them.

"Haven't you any eyes?" she said. "I can't see your eyes, snail."

"Oh, I keep them at the top of my longer pair of feelers," said the snail. "Can't you see them? Right at the top, pixie – little black things."

"Oh yes, I can see them now," said the pixie. "What a funny place to keep your eyes, snail! Why do you keep them there?"

"Well, it's rather nice to have my eyes high up on feelers I can move about here and there," said the snail. "Wouldn't *you* like eyes on the ends of movable feelers, pixie? Think what a lot you could see!"

"I should be afraid that they would get hurt, if I had them at the end of feelers," said Silky.

"Oh no!" said the snail, and he did such a funny thing. He rolled his eyes down inside his feelers, and the pixie stared in surprise.

"Oh, you can roll your eyes down your feelers, just as I pull the toe of my stocking inside out!" she said. "Sometimes I put my hand inside my stocking, catch hold of the toe, and pull it down inside the stocking, to turn it inside out – and you do the same with your eyes!"

"Yes, I do," said the snail. "It's rather a good idea, don't you think so?"

"Oh, *very* good," said Silky. "Where's your mouth? Is that it, under your feelers?"

"Yes," said the snail, and he opened it to show the pixie. She looked at it closely.

"Have you any teeth?" she said. "I have a lot."

"So have I," said the snail. "I have about fourteen thousand."

Silky stared. "You shouldn't tell silly stories like that," she said.

"I'm not telling silly stories," said the snail. "I'll show you my teeth."

He put out a long, narrow tongue, and Silky laughed. "Don't tell me that you grow teeth on your *tongue*," she said.

"Well, I do," said the snail. "Just look at my tongue, pixie. Can't you see the tiny teeth there, hundreds and hundreds of them?"

"Oh *yes*," said the pixie in surprise. "I can. They are so tiny, snail, and they all point backwards. It's like a tooth-ribbon, your tongue. How do you eat with your teeth?"

"I use my tongue like a file," said the snail. "I'll show you."

He went to a lettuce, put out his tongue, and

began to rasp away at a leaf. In a moment he had eaten quite a big piece.

"Well, you really *are* a strange creature," said Silky. She looked closely at the snail, and noticed a strange little hole opening and shutting in the top of his neck.

"What's that slit for, in your neck?" she asked. "And why does it keep opening and shutting?"

"Oh, that's my breathing-hole," said the snail. "Didn't you guess that? Every time that hole opens and shuts, I breathe."

"Why don't you breathe with your mouth, as I do?" asked Silky.

"All soft-bodied creatures like myself, that have no bones at all, breathe through our bodies," said the snail. "Now, if you will excuse me, I must get into my shell. I can see the big thrush coming."

He put his body back into his shell and stayed quite still. The thrush passed by without noticing him. The pixie went into her house, and came out with a tin of polish and a duster.

"Snail, I am going to polish up your shell for you," she said. "I shall make you look so nice. Everyone will say how beautiful you are!"

"Oh, thank you," said the snail, and he

stayed quite still whilst Silky put polish on her cloth and then rubbed his shell hard.

"I rather like that," he said.

"Well, come every day and I'll give you a good rubbing with my duster," promised the pixie.

So, very soon, the two became good friends, and the snail always came by the pixie's house for a chat whenever he was near.

One day Silky was sad. She showed the snail a necklace of bright-blue beads – but it was broken, for the clasp was lost.

"I wanted to wear this at a party tomorrow," said Silky. "But I can't get anyone to mend it for me."

"I know someone who will," said the snail. "He is a great friend of mine. He lives in a tiny house the fifth stone to the left of the old stone wall, and the fifteenth up. There's a hole there, and Mendy lives in it, doing all kinds of jobs for everyone."

"I would never find the way," said Silky. "I know I'd get lost."

"Well, I will take the necklace for you tonight," said the snail. "But I know Mendy will take a little time to do it, so you would have to fetch it yourself some time tomorrow."

"But I should get lost!" said Silky.

"I will see that you don't," said the snail. "I will take the necklace to Mendy, give it to him, and come straight back here. And behind me I will leave a silvery trail for you to follow!"

"Oh, snail, you *are* kind and clever!" said Silky, delighted. She hung the beads over the snail's feelers, and he set off towards the old wall he knew so well. It was a long way for him to go, because he travelled very slowly.

It was a dry evening and the soft body of the snail did not get along as easily as on a wet night. So he sent out some slime to help his body along, and then he glided forwards more easily.

The slimy trail dried behind him, and left a beautiful silvery path, easy to see. The snail went up the wall to the hole where old Mendy the brownie lived, and gave him the broken necklace.

"It will be ready at noon tomorrow," said Mendy. "Thank you," said the snail, and went home again, very slowly, leaving behind him a second silvery trail, running by the first.

Silky was asleep, so he didn't wake her, but he told her next morning that her necklace would be ready at noon.

"And you *can't* get lost," he said, "because I have left two silvery paths for you to follow. It doesn't matter which you walk on – either of them will lead you to Mendy."

So Silky set off on one of the silvery paths, and it led her to the old wall, up it, and into Mendy's little house. Her necklace was mended, so she put it on ready for the party. She was very pleased indeed.

"Thank you," she said. "Now I know the way to your house, I'll bring some other things for you to mend, Mendy!"

She went to find her friend, the snail. "Thank you for leaving me such a lovely silvery path," she said. "I do think you are clever!"

I expect you would like to see the snail's silvery path too, wouldn't you? Well, go round your garden any summer's morning – you are sure to see the snail's night-time trail of silver gleaming in the sunshine here and there.

Mr Topple and The Egg

MR. TOPPLE lived next door to Mr. Plod the Policeman. Mr. Topple was a brownie, and a very nice fellow too, always ready to help anyone he could.

One day his Aunt Jemima was coming to tea, and he wanted to make a little cake for her. So he got everything ready, and then, oh dear, he found that the egg in his larder was bad.

"I must have an egg for my cake," said Mr. Topple to himself. "I wonder if Mr. Plod the Policeman would sell me one. I'll ask him."

Mr. Plod kept hens in his garden, and they laid very nice eggs. Mr. Topple went to ask him, but he was out. Still, Mr. Topple knew where he would be. He would be at Busy Corner, directing the traffic there.

So off he ran to Busy Corner, and told Mr. Plod what he wanted. The big policeman nodded his head. "Of course you can have an egg from my hens. Run back, look in the hen-house, and take the biggest and brownest you see there."

So Mr. Topple went back home. He climbed over the wall and jumped down into Mr. Plod's garden. He went to the hen-house, looked round, saw one big brown egg in a nesting-box there, and came out with it in his hand.

He climbed back over the wall again, and went indoors to make his cake. He made a lovely one, and cut a big slice out of it to send to Mr. Plod for his tea.

Now, as Mr. Topple was climbing over the wall to get into Mr. Plod's garden, little Mrs Whisper was passing by. She saw him jump down, and she watched him go into the hen-house. She saw Topple come out with an egg in his hand, and jump back down over the wall into his own garden again.

"Well!" said Mrs. Whisper. "Well!" The nasty, horrid thief! He knows Mr. Plod is down at Busy Corner, and so he thought he would get over and steal an egg. Well!"

Mrs. Whisper hurried on and soon she met Mr. Talky. "Good morning, Mr. Talky," she said. "Do you know, I've just seen a most dreadful thing – I saw Mr. Topple creeping into Mr. Plod's hen-house and stealing an egg! What do you think of that?"

"What a thing to do!" said Mr. Talky,

shocked. "I'm surprised at Mr. Topple, really, I am. Dear, dear, dear – and he seems such a nice fellow too."

Mr. Talky went on his way. Soon he met Miss Simple, and he stopped to speak to her. After a bit he said, "Do you know, I've just heard a most dreadful thing. I met Mrs. Whisper and she told me that she saw Mr. Topple creeping into Mr. Plod's hen-house today and stealing an egg!"

"Well, well – would you believe it!" said Miss Simple, her eyes wide open in surprise.

"You wouldn't think Mr. Topple would do such a thing, would you?"

Miss Simple hurried on her way, longing to tell somebody about Mr. Topple. What a bit of news! Fancy Mr. Topple daring to steal an egg from the village policeman!

Miss Simple met Dame Listen. "Dame Listen!" she said at once, "I've just heard such a bit of news! Mr. Topple — you know that nice Mr. Topple the brownie, don't you — well, do you know, he's been stealing eggs out of Mr. Plod's hen-house! What do you think of that?"

"Shocking!" said Mrs. Listen. "Really shocking! Something ought to be done about it!"

She went away and soon met Mr. Meddle. She told him the news. "Mr. Meddle! Would you believe it, that brownie, Mr. Topple, is a thief! He steals eggs. Fancy that! He was seen creeping into somebody's hen-house stealing eggs! He's a thief. He ought to be in prison."

"So he ought, so he ought," said Mr. Meddle, banging his stick on the ground. "And, what's more, I shall complain about this to Mr. Plod the policeman. Why, none of our eggs or our hens either will be safe, if Mr. Topple starts stealing. There's Mr. Plod over there, at Busy Corner. I'll go and tell him now."

So Mr. Meddle, feeling very busy and important, went over to Mr. Plod. "Mr. Plod," he said, "I've a complaint to make, and I expect you to look into it. I hear that Mr. Topple is a thief. I think he ought to be in prison."

Mr. Plod was so surprised to hear this that he waved two lorries on at the same moment and there was very nearly an accident. He stared in astonishment at Mr. Meddle.

"Mr. Topple a thief!" he said. "Nonsense! I've lived next door to him for years, and a kinder, more honest fellow I never met. Who says he's a thief – and what does he steal?"

"Mrs. Listen told me," said Mr. Meddle. "She said he steals eggs."

Mr. Plod left Busy Corner, and, taking Mr. Meddle with him, walked off to find Mrs. Listen. "What's all this about Topple stealing eggs?" he said.

"Oh," said Mrs. Listen, "well, Miss Simple told me. You'd better ask her where she got the dreadful news from. There she is, in the baker's."

Mr. Plod called Miss Simple. "What's all this about Topple stealing eggs?" he said.

"Well, I heard it from Mr. Talky," said Miss Simple. "He told me all about it. Dreadful, isn't it?"

"Come along," said Mr. Plod to Mr. Meddle, Dame Listen and Sally Simple. "We'll all go to find Mr. Talky. I'm going to get to the bottom of this."

They found Mr. Talky at home. "What's all this about Topple stealing eggs?" said Mr. Plod, beginning to look rather stern.

"Isn't it a shocking thing?" said Mr. Talky. "I've told ever so many people, and they were all surprised. It was Mrs. Whisper that told me."

Mrs. Whisper lived across the road. Mr. Plod took them all to her house and banged on her door. She opened it, and looked surprised to see so many people outside.

"What's all this about Topple stealing eggs?" said Mr. Plod.

"Oh, have you heard about it?" said Mrs. Whisper. "Well – I saw him take the egg!"

"When and where?" asked Mr. Plod, taking out his note-book.

"This very morning," said Mrs. Whisper. "I was passing your backgarden, Mr. Plod, and I happened to look over the wall – and what did

I see but Mr. Topple going into your hen-house, and coming out with one of your eggs in his hand – and then he jumped back over the wall again! What do you think of that? I think he ought to be in prison."

Mr. Plod shut his note-book with a snap. He looked round so sternly that everyone began to feel afraid.

"This morning," said Mr. Plod, in a loud and angry voice, "this morning, my friend, Mr. Topple, came to me at Busy Corner, and said his aunt was coming to tea, and he was making her a cake. And as his egg was bad, could he have one of mine?"

There was silence. No one dared to say anything. Mr. Plod went on. "I said of course he could, and so, I suppose, he went back, and got the egg. And now, all round the town, there are people saying that Topple is a thief – a kind of honest fellow like Topple."

"I'm sure I'm sorry I said such a thing," began Mr. Talky, "but I believed Mrs. Whisper when she told me."

"Don't make excuses," said Mr. Plod, in a thundery sort of voice. "It's all of you who ought to be in prison, not poor Mr. Topple! How dare you say a man is a thief, Mrs.

Whisper, when you don't know at all whether he is or not? How dare you, Mr. Talky, and all you others too, repeat this wicked story, when you don't know at all whether it is true or not?"

Miss Simple began to cry. "Now, one more word of this kind from any of you, and I'll be after you!" said Mr. Plod. "You will all go round and tell everyone that you've made a sad mistake, and are ashamed of yourselves. Go now – for I've a very good mind to put you all into prison!"

Miss Simple gave a scream and ran away. The others ran too, because Mr. Plod looked so stern. "I just won't have people taking somebody's good name away!" said the policeman, and he stamped back to Busy Corner. "I just won't. It's as wicked a thing as stealing!"

Well, so it is, isn't it? I think Mrs. Whisper and the others will be very careful in future, don't you?

The Angry Pixies

THE children loved to go for a picnic in Pixie Wood. It was such a beautiful place. Primroses shone there by the hundred, violets smelt sweetly, and bluebells made a wonderful carpet in May time.

One day, when the primroses were out, Joan, Harry, Peter and Lucy went to the woods to have a picnic. They took with them packets of sandwiches and cakes, a big bar of chocolate, two bottles of lemonade, and some plastic cups to drink from.

"We shall have a lovely picnic," said Harry. "My mother has made egg and cress sandwiches."

"And mine has made jam ones," said Joan. "We can share them all out and have some of each."

They found a beautiful dell in the woods, and sat down to have their picnic. How good the food tasted. The children sat and looked round them as they ate.

Primroses shone pale and yellow all about

them. Anemones nodded in the breeze. Violets nestled close to the primroses, and birds sang all round. The green moss was as soft as smooth velvet.

A robin sat in a bush and looked at them. He was hoping for a crumb. Harry saw him. He picked up a stone and threw it at the robin.

"Don't!" said Joan. "Poor little thing – you hit it!"

The robin flew away with a cry of pain. It did not come back again. A tiny rabbit peeped at them from behind a tree. "Isn't he sweet?" said Lucy. But he didn't peep long because Peter threw a stick at him. He ran into his hole and didn't come back again.

"I've finished my dinner," said Harry. "Let's put these lemonade bottles up on that stone over there, and throw stones at them. We'll see who can break them first."

So they did. Harry was the best. He broke both bottles, and bits of glass flew all over the primroses and green moss. Peter began to throw bits of moss at the others.

"Don't" said Lucy. "Let's play a proper game, Peter. Don't let's throw any more things."

So they played "It", and in their excitement

they trampled on the primroses and violets, and crushed the anemones.

The wind came into the dell and blew the sandwich papers about. But nobody bothered to pick them up. The plastic cups were trodden on and lay in the dell too.

Soon Peter looked at his watch. "Almost time to go," he said. "Shall we dig up a few primroses to take home?"

They dug up the best ones and then they went home, thinking what a lovely picnic they had had.

Now, the next day, Harry went into the woods again. He was on his way to see his uncle, who lived on the other side of the woods. He hadn't gone very far before he heard a loud and angry voice.

"I shall tell the policeman! It's a wicked shame! I shall go and tell the policeman now!"

Harry peeped to see who was speaking. He saw a small pixie-man, and he was surprised and pleased, for he had never seen one of the little folk before.

"What's the matter?" said Harry. "Can I help you?"

"What do you think has happened?" said the pixie angrily. "I had a most beautiful home in these woods, and the prettiest garden you ever saw, with primroses, violets and anemones growing all round. And I had a robin for a friend, and a little rabbit too. I had moss for a carpet, and I kept everything as neat as could be. And now somebody has spoilt it all!"

"What a pity!" said Harry.

"Yes – they've stolen some of my primroses, trampled on all my flowers, and dug up my moss," said the pixie, angry tears running down his cheeks. "And do you know, one of them has broken my robin's leg? Think of that!"

"Oh," said Harry.

"And they frightened away my little rabbit and he won't come and talk to me," said the pixie; "but worst of all, they left broken glass all over the place, and when I got back late last night in the dark, I trod on it, cut my shoes to pieces and hurt my foot!"

Harry saw that the pixie's foot was bound up in a white rag. The little man went on, getting more and more upset as he talked.

"They left their rubbish there too – bits of paper and things like that. How dare they? What would they say if anyone did all that in *their* gardens?"

"Perhaps they didn't know it was your garden," said Harry, very red in the face.

"Well, even if they didn't, surely they had the sense to know that other people might want to come and enjoy the beauty of the woods!" cried the pixie. "Why should people spoil beautiful things? They must have very ugly minds if they can't see these woods are lovely. They must be horrid, selfish people, and I am going to the policeman who lives in the heart of the woods, to tell him to punish them. He's a pixie policeman who knows all kinds of magic. You come and tell him too."

"I must get home, thank you," said Harry, and before the pixie could say another word, he ran all the way home. He found Joan, Peter and Lucy, and told them about the angry pixie and all he had said.

"He was quite right," said Joan, looking ashamed of herself. "We did spoil that lovely dell – and oh, Harry, that poor, poor little robin! Did you really break its leg?"

Lucy had tears in her eyes. She loved birds. She didn't like to think of the frightened rabbit either. How *could* they have behaved like that?

"We'll go and tell that pixie that we're very sorry and we'll never behave like that again," said Lucy. So they all went to find him. But he wasn't there. The dell lay silent in the sunshine, spoilt and trampled.

"The pixie must have moved," said Lucy. "Let's pick up our rubbish. What a pity we can't say we're sorry and won't ever do such a thing again. I wish we could see the pixie."

But they never did. Still, they kept their word, and now, when they go for a picnic, they never spoil anything, never throw stones, and always take their rubbish back in a bag. So they should, shouldn't they?

Binky The Borrower

"PLEASE will you lend me your ladder?" said Binky the pixie, to Dame Lucy.

"Yes, but bring it back tomorrow," said Dame Lucy. Binky didn't. He stood the ladder in his shed, meaning to take it back day after day, but he didn't remember.

"Please will you lend me your barrow? Please will you lend me a book? Please will you lend me your shovel? Please will you lend me a box of matches?" Binky was always saying things like this.

The little folk of Up-and-down Village were kind and generous, so they always lent Binky the things he asked for. But he hardly ever remembered to bring them back.

"Binky! Where's my lamp?" Twinkle would shout. "I want it back!"

"Binky! Where's my carpet? Do bring it back!" Feefo would call. And Binky would always answer the same thing.

"I'll bring it back tomorrow." But he never did.

"It's too bad," grumbled the little folk of Up-and-down Village. "It's really too bad. Binky is always borrowing things and never bringing them back."

"Borrowing is not a good thing," said Feefo. "It's stealing, if the things aren't given back. It is really."

"So it is," said Twinkle. "Isn't that dreadful? Does Binky know he is a thief, if he doesn't give us back our things?"

"We'll tell him," said Dame Lucy. So they told him, and he was very upset.

"How can you say such a thing about me? You know I am a very honest pixie. I wouldn't steal for anything! I will sort out all the things I have borrowed and send them back tomorrow. I think you are all very horrid."

The next day Binky had a cold and stayed in bed, so nothing was sent back. The little folk of the village really did not know *how* to get back their things.

Then Dame Lucy had a good idea. "I'll go to my aunt, the Wise Woman, and ask her for a Get-back Spell. She knows how to make them. Then we can get back all our things!"

So off she went to the Wise Woman and asked her for a Get-back Spell. The Wise Woman gave one to her. It was in a little box. It was a yellow powder, and it had to be blown into the air when the wind was in the south.

"Say these magic words when you blow the powder," said the Wise Woman, and she told Dame Lucy some very powerful magic words. Dame Lucy hoped she would be able to remember them all.

She took the powder back to her village and showed it to everyone. "When the wind is in the south we will use it," she said. "Then all our things will come back again."

The next day the wind was in the south. Good! Dame Lucy opened the box and faced the wind. She blew the yellow powder into the breeze and then called out the magic words.

The Get-back Spell went into Binky's house. It got into everything he had ever borrowed in his life. He was most astonished when he saw his carpet get up, shake itself and rush out of the door. He was even more surprised when he saw the clock jump off the mantelpiece and the shovel hop out of the fender! They all went out of the door.

The people of the village were watching nearby to see if the Get-back Spell was going to work. As soon as they saw the carpet come

rushing out, they knew the spell was a very good one.

"Here comes my carpet!" cried Feefo, in delight, and rolled it up under his arm.

"Here's my clock!" cried Dame Lucy, and took it gladly.

"Here's my shovel!"

"Here's my lamp!"

"Here's my armchair!"

"Here's my ladder!"

One by one the things came rushing and tumbling out of Binky's house. Each one went to its owner, but some of them raced off down the road to the next village.

"Look at that," said Dame Lucy, in surprise. "I suppose those are things that Binky borrowed in the next village before he came to live here – and they are all going back to their proper owners! Good gracious, what a lot of things he has borrowed!"

He certainly had! Curtains, tables, a ladder, pails, kettles, lamps, books, pencils, a coal-scuttle, all of them came scurrying back out of Blinky's house in a great hurry to obey the Get-back Spell. The little folk began to laugh, because it really was a funny sight to see.

Binky couldn't understand what was happening. Why, all his belongings were going away! He hadn't anything left. His house was bare!

He rushed out into the street, and shouted to the others there. "What's happening? Everything has gone! My house is empty!"

"Empty!" said everyone in amazement. "What do you mean? Haven't you anything left at all?"

"Not a thing," said Binky, beginning to cry. "Oh, do tell me what's happening! Get my things back for me."

"They are not your things," said Dame Lucy, suddenly looking very stern. "They belong to others. They are the things you have borrowed. How dreadful to think that your whole house was made up of things you had borrowed!"

"Stolen, you mean!" said Feefo, fiercely. "He never meant to give them back. He's a thief! He borrows things and never returns them. That's dishonest. He's a thief!"

"I'm not, I'm not," wailed Binky, watching his pictures hop down the road to the next village. "Oh, what am I to do? Can somebody lend me a bed to sleep in and a rug to cover me?"

But nobody would. No, they knew Binky by now, and they were not going to help him to be dishonest. It would be different if he always gave back what he borrowed, but he didn't. Let him sleep out in the fields!

So he did, and then he had to go and find some work to do to buy himself the things he needed.

Wouldn't you have liked to see the Get-back Spell at work? I would!

The Birthday Party

ONCE upon a time Bron the Brownie wanted to give a birthday party.

"It shall be the most wonderful party ever given," said Bron. "I shall give it in the field that runs down to the stream, then those who want to can go for a sail in the moonlight."

"What will you have to eat," asked Jinky.

"Honey cakes, daisy-jelly, bilberry buns, and the most delicious ice-creams ever made," said Bron. "And I shall have lemonade to drink, made of dewdrops shaken off the grass."

"It does sound nice," said Tippitty.

"And I shall ask the Princess Peronel," said Bron. "She loves a party. She will be staying with her aunt, quite near here, on my birthday. I am sure she will love to come."

Everyone in Cuckoo Wood felt excited. A moonlight party near the stream, with lots of nice things to eat and drink. What fun!

Bron was very busy. He wrote out cards to tell everyone to come. He got the grey squirrel to take them to his friends, and everyone wrote back at once to say they would come.

He began to make jellies and cakes, biscuits and buns. He ordered himself a new suit of red and gold, with a pointed hat that was set with bells. "They will ring whenever I walk," said Bron. "Then people will know I am coming."

"Where will you get all the glasses and cups and plates and dishes from?" asked Tippitty. "You won't have nearly enough."

"The oak tree is giving me acorn-cups," said Bron. "I am borrowing all the other things from Jinky and Gobo – and perhaps you would lend me a few glasses, Tippitty dear."

It was to be such a big party. Bron went down to the meadow and had a look at it. He had asked all the little folk he knew – the brownies, the elves, the pixies, and a few of the nicely-behaved goblins.

"The Princess Peronel says she will come too," he told everyone. "So you must all wear your very *best* dresses and suits, and polish up your wings nicely."

"Where are you going to get all the chairs and tables you want?" asked Jinky. "I can lend you mine, Bron, but I haven't very many."

"Oh, I've thought about all that," said Bron. "I have written to the enchanter Heyho, and asked him to make me hundreds of little chairs and tables, and to send them here by midday, before the party. Then I shall have plenty of time to arrange them before midnight comes, and we begin the party."

"How is he going to send them?" asked Jinky.

"His black cats are going to bring them," said Bron. "He is going to pack them all up neatly, and put them on the backs of his big cats. Then they will bring them to me by midday. I shall arrange them in the meadow then. Won't it be fun?"

The day of the party came. Bron's new suit was ready, and his hat with little bells. He looked very fine. He hurried about, looking to see if the jellies were all right, and the lemonade was sweet enough.

Midday came – but no black cats! Bron looked out for them, and wondered why they were late. One o'clock came – two o'clock. Still no black cats with all the tables and chairs.

Then, at three o'clock, a poor, limping cat came mewing to Bron. The cat was much bigger than little Bron. He looked up at her in surprise.

"Where are the other cats?" he asked. "You

are one of Heyho's cats, aren't you? Where are the little chairs and tables you were to bring?"

"Oh, Bron, a dreadful thing happened," said the cat. "As we were going down Breezy Hill, with the piles of little chairs and tables tied safely to our backs, a big brown dog came trotting by. He saw us and chased us all."

"Oh dear! What happened?" asked Bron.

"Well, we rushed up trees," said the cat, "and all the little chairs and tables caught in the boughs and were smashed to bits. Oh, Bron, I'm so sorry."

"This is dreadful," said Bron.

"I got down the tree first, and came to tell you," said the cat. "The dog chased me again, and I hurt my paw. The other cats have gone back to our master. But he will not be able to send you any more chairs and tables in time for your party."

Bron felt as if he would burst into tears. "How can I have a party without tables and chairs?" he wailed. "I can't put the cups and plates on the ground! Oh dear, oh dear, this is a dreadful thing to happen just before the party! Whatever am I to do?"

The cat didn't know. She ran back to her master and left poor Bron looking very sad. Jinky came to see him, and he listened to the dreadful news.

"Bron – don't worry too much. I believe I know what we can do!" he said. "Let's *grow* our own tables and stools!"

"What do you mean – *grow* them?" said Bron. "I don't know enough magic for that."

"Let's put a mushroom spell on your meadow!" said Jinky. "Then mushrooms will grow up all over it."

"What's the good of that?" asked Bron. "You know what a long time plants take to grow

—weeks and weeks. Don't be silly!"

"No, Bron, no – mushrooms are not like green plants that take a long time to grow," said Jinky. "They are quite different. They grow very, very quickly – in a night! You know how quickly toadstools grow, don't you? Well, mushrooms grow very quickly too, and they have very nice broad tops that will do well for tables and stools. Do let's come and try it."

Bron began to cheer up. He went with Jinky to the meadow. Jinky began to dig about in the ground a bit, and he showed Bron some small white threads here and there. "Just a bit of mushroom magic and hundreds of mushrooms will grow!" he said.

"I don't know mushroom magic," said Bron. But Jinky did. He fetched his best wand and did a little waving and chanting. Bron thought he was really very clever.

"And now we'll just see what happens!" said Jinky, when he had finished.

Well, it really was very surprising. Before long, wherever there were the white threads that Jinky had found, the ground began to move a little, and to heave up.

"Jinky! Jinky! The mushrooms are growing!" cried Bron in delight. "Here's one – and another – and another! Oh, what fun! There will be hundreds of them. Wherever I tread I can feel them growing."

Well, by the time that it was nearly midnight, the meadow was covered with mushrooms! They grew very quickly indeed, as mushrooms always do, and Bron was full of joy when he saw what fine little tables and stools they would make.

He and Jinky and Tippitty quickly set out the goodies on the biggest mushrooms. By the time the guests arrived, everything was ready, and there was Bron, jingling his bells and giving the pretty little Princess Peronel and all his guests a great welcome!

"What marvellous tables and stools!" said the Princess. "I do like them. Aren't they nice and soft to sit on – and oh! do look underneath the tops, everyone – there are the prettiest pink frills there, as soft as silk. Bron, I think they are the nicest tables and stools I have ever seen!"

Everyone else thought so too. The tables couldn't be knocked over, because they grew from the ground. There were so many of them that everyone could sit down at once if they wanted to.

It was a splendid party. The things to eat and

drink were really lovely. There were tiny boats on the stream, made of curled-up water-lily leaves, with a white petal for a sail. The Princess had a wonderful time.

"This is the nicest party I have ever been to," she said to Bron. "The very nicest! As it is your birthday I would like to give you a present, and please wear it."

She gave him a little shiny brooch in the shape of a mushroom! She had made it by magic and Bron was very pleased with it. "I shall always remember this party when I wear it," he said. "Thank you, Princess Peronel."

At dawn the guests all went home. Jinky and Bron cleared away the dishes and cups. Only the mushroom stools and tables were left.

"It's a pity they will all be wasted," said Bron. "They are so pretty, with their frills underneath, and they smell so nice!"

But they were not wasted – for, when the little folk were all sound asleep in the early morning sun, children came into the fields with baskets.

"Mushrooms!" they cried. "Mushrooms for breakfast! Oh look! There are hundreds, all with pretty frills, and nice white caps. Mushrooms! Mushrooms!"

They picked them all – and for their breakfast

they ate the stools and tables that the little folk had grown so quickly the night before. They *did* enjoy them!

It's strange that mushrooms and toadstools always grow so quickly, isn't it? There must be some of Jinky's magic about!

He Wouldn't Take the Trouble

OH-DEAR, the Brownie, was cross.

"I ordered two new tyres for my old bicycle ages ago," he said, "And they haven't come yet! So I have to walk to the village and back each day, instead of riding. It's such a nuisance."

"It won't hurt you," said a friend Feefo. "Don't make such a fuss, Oh-Dear! Everything is so much trouble to you, and you sigh and groan too much."

Feefo was right. Oh-Dear did make a fuss about everything. If his chimney smoked and needed sweeping he almost cried with rage –though if he had had it swept as soon as it began to smoke, his rooms wouldn't have got so black.

If his hens didn't lay eggs as often as they should, he shouted angrily at them – but if only he had bothered to feed them properly at the right times, he would have got all the eggs he wanted.

Now he was angry because his new bicycle

tyres hadn't come. It was really most annoying.

The next day he walked down into the village again to ask at the post-office if his tyres had come. But they hadn't. "They might arrive by the next post," said the little postmistress. "If they do, I will send them by the carrier."

"Pooh – you always say that – and they never do come!" said Oh-Dear rudely. He walked out of the shop. It was his day for going to see his old aunt Chuckle. He didn't like her very much because she laughed at him – but if he didn't go to see her she didn't send him the cakes and pies he liked so much.

Oh-Dear walked in at his aunt's gate. He didn't bother to shut it, so it banged to and fro in the wind and his aunt sent him out to latch it.

"You just don't take the trouble to do anything," she said. "You don't bother to shine your shoes each morning – just look at them –and you don't trouble to post the letters I give you to post – and you don't even take the trouble to say thank-you for my pies and cakes. You are so lazy, Oh-Dear!"

"Oh Dear!" said Oh-Dear, sulking. "Don't scold me again. You are always scolding me."

"Well, you always need it," said his aunt, and laughed at his sulking face. "Now cheer up,

Oh-Dear – I've a little bit of good news for you."

"What is it?" said Oh-Dear.

"I've heard from my friend, Mr. Give-a-Lot, and he is having a party tomorrow," said Aunt Chuckle. "He said that if you like to go, he will be very pleased. So go, Oh-Dear, because you love parties, and you know that Mr. Give-a-Lot always has a lovely tea, and everyone goes away with a nice present."

"Oh!" said Oh-Dear, pleased – but then his face grew gloomy. "I can't go. It's too far to walk. No bus goes to Mr. Give-a-Lot's – and I haven't got my new bicycle tyres so I can't ride there. Oh dear, oh dear, oh dear – isn't that just my luck?"

"Well – never mind," said Aunt Chuckle. "I should have thought you could walk there – but if it's too far, it's a pity. Cheer up. Look in the oven and you'll see a pie there."

Oh-Dear stayed with his aunt till after tea. Then he set out to walk home. It was quite a long way. He groaned.

"Oh dear! It will be dark before I get home. Oh dear! What a pity I can't go to that party tomorrow. Oh dear, why isn't there a bus at this time to take me home?"

He went down the hill. A cart passed him and bumped over a hole in the road. Something fell out of the cart and rolled to the side of the road.

"Hi, hi!" shouted Oh-Dear, but the driver didn't hear him. "Now look at that!" said Oh-Dear, crossly. "I suppose I ought to carry the parcel down the road and catch the cart up – or take it to the police-station."

He picked up the parcel. It was too dark to see the name and address on it, but it was very heavy and awkward to carry.

"I can't be bothered to go after the cart or carry this all the way to the police-station!" said Oh-Dear to himself. "I really can't. And what's more I won't. Somebody else can have the trouble of taking it along!"

He threw the parcel down at the side of the road and went on his way. He wasn't going to take the trouble of finding out who it belonged to, or of handing it over safely. There the parcel lay all night, and all the next morning, for no one came by that way for a long time.

About three o'clock Cherry the pixie came along. She saw the parcel and picked it up. "Oh!" she said, "This must have been dropped by the carrier's cart yesterday. Somebody didn't get their parcel. I wonder who it was."

She looked at the name and address on it. "Master Oh-Dear, the Pixie," she read. "Lemon Cottage, Breezy Corner. Oh, it must be the bicycle tyres that Oh-Dear has been expecting for so long. Well – the parcel is very heavy, but I'll carry it to him myself."

So the kind little pixie took it along to Oh-Dear's cottage and gave it to him. "I found it lying in the road," she said. "It must have dropped off the carrier's cart last night."

"Yes, I saw it," said Oh-Dear, "but I wasn't

going to be bothered to carry it all the way after the cart."

"But Oh-Dear – it's for you," said Cherry, in surprise. "I suppose it was too dark for you to see the name on it. It's your very own parcel – I expect it's the tyres you wanted."

"Gracious! It is!" said Oh-Dear, in excitement. "Perhaps I can go to Mr. Give-a-Lot's party after all."

He tore off the paper and took off the lid of a big cardboard box. Inside were all the things he had ordered for his bicycle – two new tyres, a pump, a basket and a lamp.

Oh-Dear rushed to put them on his bicycle. He forgot to thank Cherry for her kindness. He worked hard at fitting on his tyres, but it was very very difficult.

At last he had them on – but when he looked at the clock, it was half-past six! Too late to go to the party now!

"Oh dear, isn't that just my bad luck!" wailed Oh-Dear. "Why didn't you bring me the parcel earlier, Cherry?"

"Why didn't you take the trouble to see to it yourself last night, when you saw it in the road!" said Cherry. "Bad luck, indeed –nothing of the sort. It's what you deserve! You won't bother yourself about anything, you just won't take the trouble – and now you've punished yourself, and a VERY GOOD THING TOO!"

She went out and banged the door. Oh-Dear sat down and cried. Why did he always have such bad luck, why, why, why?

Well, I could tell him the reason why, just as Cherry did, couldn't you?

A Puddle for the Donkeys

ONE day Dame Bonnet set out to catch the bus to the market. And, at the same time, Dame Two-Shoes set out to get the bus, too. They met on the common that leads down to where the big green bus stops three times a day.

"Good day to you, Dame Bonnet," said Dame Two-Shoes. "And where are you off to this fine morning?"

To the market to buy me a good fat donkey," said Dame Bonnet.

"What a strange thing!" said Dame Two-Shoes. "I'm going to market to buy the very same thing."

"Well, well, there will be plenty of good fat donkeys for sale," said Dame Bonnet. "Will you ride home on yours?"

"That I will," said Dame Two-Shoes. "I'm taking the morning's bus there, but I'm riding home on my own donkey, so I am."

"And that's what I shall do, too," said Dame Bonnet. "I'm taking a carrot for my good donkey. Look!"

"Well, well, how do we think alike!" said Dame Two-Shoes, and she held out a large carrot, too. "I've got a carrot as well."

"I expect our donkeys will be thirsty this hot day," said Dame Bonnet, looking round. "There's a nice big puddle near here, left by the rain. I mean to let my donkey drink it up."

The two old dames looked at the puddle of water. "I had that idea, too," said Dame Two-Shoes, frowning. "That puddle is only enough for one donkey. You must let mine share it, or mine will have none. Let them have half each. That will be fair."

"If my donkey is here first, he shall have all the puddle," said Dame Bonnet at once. "I spoke about it first."

"Don't be so mean," cried Dame Two-Shoes. "Would you have my donkey die of thirst?"

"Well, I shall not let mine die of thirst, either," said Dame Bonnet. "I don't care about yours. I have to think of my own good fat donkey. I don't go to market to buy donkeys and then let them die of thirst on the way home. The puddle is for my own donkey. So make up your mind about that!"

The old horse who lived on the common

came wandering by, wondering why the old dames were talking so loudly. He saw the gleaming puddle of water and went over to it.

"Now look here!" said Dame Two-Shoes, angrily. "For the last time, Dame Bonnet, will you let my donkey share that puddle? For the last time I ask you."

"And for the last time I say that I shall look after my own good fat donkey, and not yours," said Dame Bonnet, in a rage.

Then they heard the sound of gulping, and they turned to see what it was. It was the old horse drinking up every scrap of the puddle. There wasn't a drop left at all.

"Look at that!" cried Dame Two-Shoes in a fine old temper. "That greedy horse has been drinking up our donkeys' puddle! You bad horse!"

"Who do you belong to?" said Dame Bonnet. "I'll go and tell your master. That puddle belonged to our two good fat donkeys. Now, when we ride them home tonight, there will be no puddle for them to drink and they will both die of thirst."

"Hrrrumph!" said the horse, and backed away in alarm.

There came the sound of rumbling wheels and

the old dames looked down to the road at the bottom of the common.

"The bus, it's the bus!" they cried. "It's coming! Hurry, hurry! We shall never get to the market in time!"

So off they ran over the common path, the old horse looking after them in astonishment. How they ran! They panted and they puffed, they pulled their skirts away from the prickly gorse bushes and tried to hold them, they skipped over the rabbit-holes, and ran like two-year-olds.

The bus stopped. Nobody got out. Nobody got in. The driver looked round, but didn't see Dame Bonnet and Dame Two-Shoes scurrying along.

They had no breath left to shout at him. They ran and ran. But the bus went off without them, down the country road, out of sight.

"Oh!" said Dame Bonnet, almost in tears. "Now we can't get to the market in time."

"We can't buy our donkeys," said Dame Two-Shoes. "We shall have to walk home," said Dame Bonnet.

"If we hadn't quarrelled about the pool of water that isn't there, we should be halfway to market now, we should buy good fat donkeys, and we should ride home on them," wept Dame Two-Shoes.

"And we would have given them a drink before we started so that they wouldn't have wanted the puddle at all," said Dame Bonnet.

They went slowly back home again. The old horse saw them and stared after them.

"Now what do they want with donkeys?" he said to himself. "Donkeys themselves, that's what they are! Hrrrumph!"

And I rather think he was right.

The Very Lovely Pattern

BETTY was sitting in her seat at school, trying very hard to think of a lovely pattern to draw and colour.

"I'm no good at drawing," said Betty to herself. "Not a bit of good! I never shall be. But oh, I do wish I could think of a pattern to draw on this page, so that Miss Brown would be pleased with me!"

"Betty! Are you dreaming as usual?" said Miss Brown. "Do get on with your work."

"I'm trying to think of a pattern," said Betty. "But it's very hard."

"No, it isn't. It's easy," said Harry. "Look, Betty – do you see my pattern? I've made a whole row of little rounds, with squares inside them, and I am going to colour the square yellow, and the bits inside the rounds are going to be blue. It will be a lovely pattern when it's finished. I shall make it all over the page."

"Yes – it *is* lovely!" said Betty. "I think I'll do that pattern too!"

"No," said Harry. "You mustn't. It's *my*

pattern, the one *I* thought of. You mustn't copy."

"No, you must think of one for yourself," said Peggy. "Look at mine, Betty. Do you like it?"

Betty looked at Peggy's. She had drawn a pattern of ivy-leaves all over her page, joining them together with stalks. It was really lovely.

"Oh dear – I do, *do* wish I could think of a lovely pattern too," said Betty.

But do you know, by the end of the lesson poor Betty still sat with an empty page before her! She hadn't drawn anything. Miss Brown was cross.

"That is really naughty, Betty," she said. "You must take your pattern book home with you, and think of a pattern to bring me tomorrow morning. You have wasted half an hour."

Betty was very upset. She badly wanted to cry. She worked very hard in the next lesson, but all the time she was thinking of whether or not she would be able to bring Miss Brown a lovely pattern the next day. She was sure she wouldn't be able to.

"It's snowing!" said Harry suddenly. "Oh, Miss Brown, look – it's snowing!"

Everyone looked out of the window. Big white snow-flakes came floating down without a sound.

"The snow is so quiet," said Betty. "That's what I love so much about it."

"It will be lovely to go home in the snow," said Harry. "Miss Brown, isn't it fun to look up into the sky when it is snowing and see millions and millions of snow-flakes coming down? Where do they come from?"

"Well," said Miss Brown, "when the clouds float through very cold air, they become frozen. Sometimes, you know, the clouds turn into rain-drops. But when there is frost about, they turn into tiny ice-crystals instead – and these join together and make a big snowflake. It has to fall down, because light though it is, it is too heavy to float in the sky."

"Snow-flakes look like pieces of cloud," said Harry. "Bits of frozen mist – how lovely!"

Betty thought it was lovely too. As she went home through the snow, she looked up into the sky. It was full of falling flakes, silent and slow and beautiful.

The little girl lost her way in the snow. She suddenly knew she was lost, and she leaned against a tree and began to cry.

"What's the matter?" said a little voice, and Betty saw a small man, dressed just like a brownie, all in brown from top to toe.

"Everything's gone wrong today!" said Betty, sobbing. "I've lost my way in the snow – and Miss Brown was very cross with me because I couldn't think of a pattern."

"What sort of pattern?" asked the brownie in surprise. "Why do you have to think of patterns?"

Betty told him. "It's something we do at school. We make up our own patterns, draw them and colour them. It's fun to do it if you are clever at thinking of patterns. But I'm not."

"But why do you bother to think of them?" asked the brownie. "There are lovely patterns all round you. A daisy-flower makes a lovely pattern – so does a pretty oak-leaf."

"There aren't any daisies or oak-leaves about now," said Betty. "I can't copy those."

"Well, look – you've got a most wonderful pattern on your sleeve!" said the brownie suddenly. "Look! Look!"

Betty saw a snow-flake caught on the sleeve of her black coat. She looked at it hard.

"Have you got good eyes?" said the brownie. "Can you see that the snow-flake is made up of tiny crystals – oh, *very* tiny?"

"Yes, I can," said Betty, looking hard. "Oh, what lovely patterns they are, brownie! Oh, I do wish I could see them get bigger!"

"I'll get my magic glass for you," said the brownie, and he suddenly opened a door in a tree, went inside, and hopped out again with a round glass that had a handle.

"It's a magnifying glass," said Betty. "My granny has one when she wants to read the newspaper. She holds it over the print and it makes all the letters look big, so that she can easily read them."

"Well, this will make the snow-crystals look much bigger to you," said the brownie. He held the glass over Betty's black sleeve – and the little girl cried out in delight.

"Oh! Oh! They are beautiful! Oh, Brownie, they are the loveliest shapes!"

"But they are all alike in one way, although they are all quite different," said the brownie. "Look at them carefully, and count how many sides each little crystal has got, Betty."

Betty counted. "How funny! They all have six sides!" she said. "All of them. Not one of them has four or five or seven sides – they all have six!"

"Ice-crystals always do," said the brownie. "But although they always have to have six sides, you won't find one ice-crystal that is like another. They all grow into a different six-sided pattern. Isn't that marvellous?"

"It's like magic," said Betty. "Just like magic. Oh – the snowflake has melted into water! The ice-crystals have gone. Quick – I want to see some more. I'll catch another snow-flake on my black sleeve."

Soon she was looking at yet more tiny crystals through the glass. They all had six sides, each one was different and they were beautiful.

"Brownie," said Betty suddenly, "I shall choose these ice-crystals for the pattern I have to do for Miss Brown. Oh, they will make a most wonderful pattern! I can make a different pattern for every page in my drawing book —patterns much lovelier than any of the other children draw. Oh, I do feel excited!"

"I'll show you the way home," said the brownie. "I'm glad you are pleased about the ice-crystals. It's funny you didn't know about them. You'll be able to make fine patterns now!"

Betty went home. She thought of the lovely six-sided crystals she had seen, and she began to draw them very carefully.

She drew a page of this pattern. Then she turned over and drew a page of a second pattern, choosing another ice-crystal whose shape she remembered.

Mother came to see. "Betty, what a lovely pattern!" she said. "Quite perfect! How *did* you think of it!"

"I didn't," said Betty. "I saw it on my black sleeve, out in the snow. It's a six-sided ice-crystal, Mother. Oh, Mother, where is Granny's magnifying glass? Do take it out into the snow and look through it at a snow-flake on your sleeve! Then you will see how different all the ice-crystals are – and yet each one has six sides. There is no end to the shapes and patterns they make."

Miss Brown was full of surprise when she saw Betty's patterns the next day. "You didn't do these, dear, surely!" she said. "Why, even I couldn't think of patterns like this. They are wonderful."

"I'll show you where to find them," said Betty happily. "It's snowing, Miss Brown. Come out with me – and all the others too – and I'll show you where I found these beautiful patterns!"

She took them out into the snow, and they saw what she had seen. You will want to see it too, of course. So remember, next time it snows, go out with a bit of black cloth and catch a snow-flake. You'll get such a surprise when you see the beautiful six-sided crystals in the flake.

Dame Lucky's Umbrella

DAME Lucky had a nice yellow umbrella that she liked very much. It had a strange handle. It was in the shape of a bird's head, and very nice to hold.

Dame Lucky had had it for her last birthday. Her brother had given it to her. "Now don't go lending this to anyone," he said. "You're such a kindly, generous soul that you will lend anything to anyone. But this is such a nice umbrella that I shall be very sad if you lose it."

"I won't lose it," said Dame Lucky. "I shall be very, very careful with it. It's the nicest one I've ever had."

She used it two or three times in the rain and was very pleased with it because it opened out big and wide and kept every spot of rain from her clothes.

Then the summer came and there was no rain to bother about for weeks. Dame Lucky put her umbrella safely away in her wardrobe.

One morning in September her friend, Mother Lucy, came to see her. "Well, well, this *is* a surprise," said Dame Lucky. "You've been so ill that I never thought you'd be allowed to come all this way to see me!"

"Oh, I'm much better," said Mother Lucy. "I mustn't stay long, though, because I have to get on to my sister's for lunch. She's expecting me in half an hour."

But when Mother Lucy got up to go she looked at the sky in dismay. "Oh, goodness –it's just going to pour with rain. Here are the first drops. I haven't brought an umbrella with me and I shall get soaked."

"Dear me, you mustn't get wet after being so ill," said Dame Lucky at once. "You wait a moment. I'll get my new umbrella. But don't lose it, Lucy, because it's the only one I have and it's very precious."

"Thank you. You're a kind soul," said Mother Lucy. Dame Lucky fetched the yellow umbrella and put it up for her. Then off went Mother Lucy to her sister's, quite dry in the pouring rain.

She had a nice lunch at her sister's – and, will you believe it, when she left she quite forgot to take Dame Lucky's umbrella with her because it had stopped raining and the sun was shining!

So there it stood in the umbrella-stand, whilst Mother Hannah waved goodbye to her sister Lucy.

In a little while it began to pour with rain again. Old Mr. Kindly had come to call on Mother Hannah without an umbrella and he asked her to lend him one when he was ready to go home.

"You may take any of the umbrellas in the stand," said Mother Hannah. "There are plenty there."

So what did Mr. Kindly do but choose the yellow umbrella with the bird-handle, the one that belonged to Dame Lucky! Off he went with it, thinking what a fine one it was and how well it kept the rain off.

When he got home his little grand-daughter was there, waiting for him. "Oh, Granddad! Can you lend me an umbrella?" she cried. "I've come out without my mackintosh and Mummy will be cross if I go home wet."

"Yes, certainly," said Mr. Kindly. "Take this one. I borrowed it from Mother Hannah. You can take it back to her tomorrow."

Off went Little Corinne, the huge umbrella almost hiding her. Her mother was out when she got in, so she stood the umbrella in the hall-stand and went upstairs to take off her things.

Her brother ran down the stairs as she was about to go up. "Hallo, Corinne! Is it raining? Blow, I'll have to take an umbrella, then!"

And, of course, he took Dame Lucky's, putting it up as soon as he got out of doors. Off he went, whistling in the rain, to his friend's house.

He put the umbrella in the hall-stand and went to find Jacko, his friend. Soon they were fitting together their railway lines, and when Pip said goodbye to Jacko he quite forgot about the umbrella because the sun was now shining again.

So there it stayed in Jacko's house all night. His Great-aunt Priscilla saw it there the next morning and was surprised because she hadn't seen it before. Nobody knew who owned it. What a peculiar thing!

Now, two days later, Dame Lucky put on her things to go out shopping and visiting. She looked up at the sky as she stepped out of her front door.

"Dear me – it looks like rain!" she said. "I must take my umbrella."

But it wasn't in the hall-stand. And it wasn't in the wardrobe in her bedroom, either. How strange! Where could it be?

"I must have lent it to somebody," said Dame Lucky. "I've forgotten who, though. Oh dear, I do hope I haven't lost it for good!"

She set out to do her shopping. It didn't rain whilst she was at the market. "Perhaps it won't rain at all," thought Dame Lucky. "I'll visit my old friend Priscilla on my way back."

She met Jacko on the way. "Is your Great-aunt Priscilla at home?" she asked him.

"Oh, yes," said Jacko. "She was only saying today that she wished she could see you. You go in and see her, Dame Lucky. You might just get there before the rain comes?"

She went on to the house where her friend Priscilla lived. She just got there before the rain fell. Dame Priscilla was very pleased to see her.

Soon they were sitting talking over cups of cocoa.

"Well, I must go," said Dame Lucky at last. "Oh dear – look at the rain! And I don't have an umbrella!"

"What! Have you lost yours?" asked Priscilla. "How unlucky! Well, I'll lend you one."

She took Dame Lucky to the hall-stand and Dame Lucky looked at the two or three umbrellas standing there. She gave a cry.

"Why! Where did *this* one come from? It's mine, I do declare! Look at the bird-handle! Priscilla, however did it come here?"

"Nobody knows," said Dame Priscilla in astonishment. "Is it really yours? Then *how* did it get here? It has been here for the last two days!"

"Waiting for me, then, I excpect," said Dame Lucky happily. "Isn't that a bit of luck, Priscilla? I shan't need to borrow one from you. I'll just take my *own* umbrella! Goodbye!"

Off she went under the great yellow umbrella, very pleased to have it again. And whom should she meet on her way home but her brother, the very one who had given her the umbrella!

"Hallo, hallo!" he cried. "I see you still have your umbrella! I *would* have been cross if you'd lost it. Let me share it with you!"

So they walked home together under the big yellow umbrella – and to this day Dame Lucky doesn't know how it came to be standing in Dame Priscilla's hall-stand, waiting for her.

The Yellow Motor Car

BRIAN had a yellow motor car, just big enough to take his teddy bear for a drive. It was a clockwork car, and Brian had to wind it up with a large key. It said, "Urrr, urrrr, urrrr" whenever it was wound up. It ran quickly across the floor, from end to end of the big nursery, and looked really fine.

It hadn't a hooter. It hadn't a brake. Its lamps were only pretend ones, with no glass and, of course, Brian couldn't switch them on, because they were only pretend-lamps. Still, they looked very fine.

Now one night a surprising thing happened to Brian. He was awakened by somebody pulling so hard at his sheet that the bedclothes nearly came off the bed. Brian sat up, quite cross.

"Who's pulling off the clothes! Stop, please!"

And then a small, growly voice spoke rather humbly to him.

"Brian! It's Bruiny, your teddy bear. Please

wake up and come into the nursery very quietly. Something's happened."

"Are you real, or am I dreaming that you are walking and talking?" Brian asked.

"You're not dreaming," said the bear. "Oh, do come, Brian. The King of the Brownies is in the nursery and he is getting so cross."

"Good gracious!" said Brian, more astonished than ever. "The King of the Brownies! I can't believe it! I'm just coming – where are my slippers?"

He went into the nursery with the bear.

Bruiny pulled at his pyjamas to make him go more quickly, and there he saw a most peculiar sight.

A small man with a long beard was pacing up and down the nursery, muttering to himself. He wore brown and green clothes, and a small golden crown. Beside him, trying to calm him down, were two more brownies.

"I tell you, it was a great mistake to get the black bats to draw my carriage!" shouted the King in a high, squeaky voice. "What happens? They see flying beetles, go after them, turn upside down to catch them, and I am flung out of my carriage, bumpity-bump!"

"Well, Your Majesty, it's a good thing you were not hurt," said the little servants, hurrying beside him as he paced up and down the nursery carpet.

"Hurt! I don't mind being hurt! What I do mind is that those stupid, silly, tiresome bats have gone off to eat their beetles and taken my carriage with them! And how I am going to get to the Pixie's Ball by midnight, I do *not* know! I, who have never been half a minute late for anything in all my life!" The brownie king stamped on the floor, took off his crown, and flung it down.

The servants picked it up, dusted it, and put it back on his head. All the toys watched, quite frightened, for they had never seen such an angry person before. Brian stared in surprise. The king was so small, so fierce, and so very surprising.

"Well! Anyone any suggestions to make?" stormed the brownie king, looking round at his servants and the toys. "Isn't there a toy train I can ride to the ball in? Or a toy aeroplane I can fly off in?"

"Please, Your Majesty, the train is broken, and the aeroplane won't fly," said the teddy bear. "But look, I've brought you Brian. I thought maybe he could help you."

The brownie king saw Brian for the first time. He bowed, and so did Brian. Then the king flew off into a temper again.

"It's too bad!" he squeaked, in his funny high voice. "I can't go to the ball, and if I do I'll be late. Oh, I'm so annoyed!"

He took off his crown again and flung it down on the floor. The servants picked it up at once. Brian really couldn't help smiling.

"Now look here," he said. "I've thought of something that might help. I've a toy motor car that would just about fit you and your servants.

Look, here it is. Would you like to go to the ball in it?"

The king looked at it. He screwed up his nose. He frowned.

"No lights," he said. "No brake. No hooter. Silly sort of car this!"

"Well, it's only a toy one you know," said Brian. "I wish it *had* got a real hooter, and brake, and lamps. But toy cars like this never do have them."

"A little magic would put that right," said the teddy bear to the king.

"Of course, of course!" said the king. He took a wand from his pocket and waved it over the car, touching the lamps, the steering-wheel, and the inside of the car. And at once there was a small hooter on the wheel, a brake inside the car, and the lamps shone! Just like a real car!

Brian's heart beat fast. This was very exciting indeed. Still grumbling, the brownie king got into the yellow toy motor car and took the wheel. The servants wound it up with the key. "Urrr, urrrrrrr, urrrr!" it went.

The car shot across the floor, with the lamps shining brightly, hooted loudly at the clock-work mouse who was in the way, and disappeared out of the door! Brian heard it go down the passage, and hoped that the garden-door was open.

"Well," he said, "that was a very funny thing to happen in the middle of the night! I do hope I'll get my car back again all right."

"Of course you will," said Bruiny. "No doubt about that at all. What a temper the brownie king has, hasn't he? Flinging his crown about like that! Well, you'd better go back to bed, Brian. You must be tired. Thank you so much for your help."

Brian did go back to bed, for he was dreadfully sleepy. And in the morning, of course, he was certain that it was all a dream.

But do you know, when he got out his toy yellow motor car to play with it, it had a hooter, a brake, and the lamps were real! There was a tiny switch by the steering-wheel that turned them off and on. Brian could hardly believe his eyes.

And now when his friends come to tea they have great fun with that yellow motor car. They put Bruiny into the car, wind it up, and send it off with the lamps alight. Bruiny is *very* clever at hooting and putting on the brake – you should just see him!

The Little Hidden Spell

ONCE upon a time Jinky came running into Tiptoe's cottage in great excitement.

"What's the matter?" asked Tiptoe. "You do look pleased."

"Well, I am," said Jinky. "What do you think? I have made a most wonderful spell! It is a spell that will make sad people smile – and, as you know, anyone who can be made to smile does not feel so sad! Isn't that marvellous?"

"Yes, it is," said Tiptoe. "Where is the spell? Show it to me."

Jinky took it out of his pocket. It was so small that it looked no bigger than a poppy seed. It was bright blue, and twinkled as Jinky held it in his hand.

"That's all it is," he said. "Just that. But if any sad person holds it in his hand for just one second, he will smile at once."

"Be careful that Tangle the goblin doesn't hear of it," said Tiptoe. "He would take it away from you and sell it to Tall-Hat the enchanter for a lot of money."

"I'm afraid Tangle does know about it," said
Jinky. "You see, Tiptoe, I was so pleased that
I couldn't help making up a little song about
my new spell – and I sang it on the way here."

"Oh dear – and I suppose Tangle heard it,"
said Tiptoe sadly. "Oh, Jinky – quick – here
comes Tangle now! I am sure he is after your
new spell. Hide it quickly!"

"Where? Where?" cried Jinky.

"It's no good putting it into my pocket, no
good at all. He'd find it there!"

Tiptoe picked up a bag from the table. In it

were a good many little brown things. She picked one out and gave it to Jinky.

"Stuff the spell in one of these tiny bulbs," she said. "Go on, hurry! Stuff it right down at the top end. That's right."

"I am sure Tangle would never think of looking there," said Jinky. "I'll put the little bulb in my pocket, and I'll bury it deep in my garden, Tiptoe. Then no one will know where it is but me. I can dig it up when Tangle has forgotten about it, can't I?"

"Yes," said Tiptoe. "Ah – here he is!"

Tangle walked into Tiptoe's kitchen. He was called Tangle because his hair always wanted brushing and combing. He was a very untidy goblin.

"Where's this spell I heard you singing about?" he said to Jinky.

"Spell? What spell?" said Jinky, opening his eyes very wide.

"It's no good pretending to me that you don't know about the smiling-spell," said Tangle angrily. "I know you brought it to show Tiptoe."

He caught hold of poor Jinky and put his hand into every one of Jinky's pockets. He found a red handkerchief, an old bit of toffee, a piece of string, two stones with little holes in them – and the tiny bulb.

"What's this?" said Tangle, holding it up.

"That's one of my snowdrop bulbs," said Tiptoe, showing Tangle the bag of them. "I'm going to plant them under my lilac tree. I gave Jinky one for himself."

Tangle gave Jinky back all the things he had taken from his pocket. Then he searched Tiptoe's kitchen well, even looking into her two teapots. She was very cross.

"You've no right to do this!" she said to Tangle. "No right at all. I shall never, never ask you to come to any of my parties."

"Pooh! I don't like parties," said Tangle. He went off in a temper, and banged the kitchen door so hard that a plate fell off the dresser and broke.

"Horrid thing!" said Tiptoe, almost in tears. "Look – now he's peeping in at the window! Jinky, don't take the spell out of the bulb, whatever you do, or he'll see it. Hurry home, and bury it in your garden tonight, when it's dark and Tangle won't see you."

Jinky waited until Tangle had gone away. Then he hurried home as fast as he could. He didn't sing any song about his smiling-spell as he went. He ran indoors and shut and bolted his door.

Tangle came along, but Jinky wouldn't open his door, so Tangle had to go away. That night, when it was dark, Jinky opened his door and crept softly outside.

He went to his big garden, and found a trowel. He dug a little hole, popped the snowdrop bulb into it, and covered it with soil.

"Now I've hidden my spell, and no one will know where it is!" thought Jinky to himself.

Now, soon after that, Tangle went away to live somewhere else. Jinky was delighted.

"Now I can dig up my smiling-spell again, and use it!" he said. So out he went and got his trowel.

But dear me, he couldn't think where he had put the little bulb! He stood there in the middle of his big garden and frowned hard.

"Did I put it by the wall over there? Or did I put it under the hedge? Or could I have put it into the rose-bed?"

He didn't know. He began to dig here and there, but he couldn't find it. It was no good trying to hunt for it. He might have to dig up the whole garden before he found it!

"Oh dear!" said Jinky, very sad. "Now I've

lost it. I shall never find it again. My wonderful, marvellous smiling-spell is gone, quite gone!"

He went to tell Tiptoe. But she didn't seem at all sad. She smiled so widely that Jinky wondered if someone had given *her* a smiling-spell to hold in her hand for a second.

"Don't worry, Jinky dear," she said. "You will find your spell again in the early springtime. It's only just past Christmas now – you wait for a few weeks, and you will find your spell. I promise you that!"

"But how can I find it?" asked Jinky. Tiptoe wouldn't tell him.

"I've always told you that you are very, very stupid about things like seeds and flowers and bulbs and trees," she said. "You don't know anything about them at all, and it is very wrong of you. You have a lovely big garden, Jinky, and yet you don't grow anything in it but grass and weeds!"

"Just tell me how I can find my wonderful spell again," said Jinky. "Please do, Tiptoe."

"If you knew anything at all about plants, I wouldn't need to tell you!" laughed Tiptoe. "Now go away, Jinky, and watch your garden well this spring-time. If you see anything strange in it, come and tell me."

Jinky watched his garden, as Tiptoe had told him. It was bare and brown in January. At the beginning of February there came a little snowfall. It made the garden look very pretty. Jinky went out to look at it.

And then he saw two straight green leaves growing up from the earth beneath the snow. He saw a tight little bud pushing up between the two leaves. He was astonished.

"A flower so early in the year!" he said. "How lovely! I must watch it."

So he watched it each day. He saw the flower-stalk grow long. He watched the bud shake itself free of its covering and droop its pretty head. He saw the flower open into a pure-white bell, its three outer petals as white as snow itself.

He went to tell Tiptoe. She smiled. "I thought you would soon be coming to tell me about the snowdrop," she said. She put on her hat and went back to Jinky's garden with him. "Yes – that's the snowdrop which is growing from the tiny brown bulb you buried," she said. "You buried your spell – but you planted a snowdrop, Jinky! And it grew, as you see!"

"How can it grow in such cold weather?" said Jinky, amazed. "Where have the leaves come from, and the beautiful flower?"

"Out of the bulb!" said Tiptoe. "The bulb is a little store-house of food, Jinky. It can send up leaves and flowers very early in the year. When the flower has faded, dig up the old bulb – and you will find your spell still there in safety!"

So Jinky waited till the pretty flower had died, and then he carefully dug up the old bulb, which by now was dried up, because the growing leaves and flowers had used up the food it had held. In it was still his wonderful spell. He took it out, twinkling blue, and ran off to Tiptoe with it.

"I shall sell my spell to a doctor for a lot of money!" he cried. "And, Tiptoe, with some of the money I shall buy hundreds and hundreds of bulbs! I shall plant them in my garden – and then, early in the year, I shall have the joy of seeing them grow!"

"Get daffodils and hyacinths too," said Tiptoe, smiling. "They all store up food in their bulbs, and send up leaves and flowers early in the year."

"I think a bulb is just as much a magic thing as my smiling-spell," said Jinky.

And I really think he was right! Can you plant a bulb and watch it send up leaves and flowers? You will think it is like magic too.

(If you would like to see how a bulb is made, get an onion, cut it in half, and have a look at it.)

The Forgotten Pets

EILEEN and Fred had a good many pets, but they didn't love them very much. They had a rabbit in a big hutch. They had a yellow canary in a cage. They had a dog and a nice kennel for it. But not one of the pets was happy.

"My hutch smells," said the rabbit. "It hasn't been cleaned out for days!"

"I haven't any water in my pot, in my pot, in my pot," trilled the canary. "Eileen has forgotten again."

"I want warm straw in my kennel because the nights are cold," barked the dog. "Wuff, wuff – bring me warm straw!"

But the children didn't look after their pets as they should, because they didn't love them. They shouldn't have had pets, of course, because they weren't the right kind of children for them.

One day the rabbit sent a message to a pixie friend of his. "Come and help me. I am unhappy. The children who own me don't look after me at all."

The pixie went to two or three of his friends, and they made a plan. The next day, when the two children were coming back from school, the pixies met them.

"Would you come and stay with us for a day or two?" said Twinkle, the chief pixie. "We don't see many little boys and girls in Fairyland, and we would like to give you a little house to stay in, and we would be so glad if you would let all the fairies, pixies and brownies have a look at you."

The children thought this sounded lovely. "Yes," said Eileen, "of course we'll come. Fancy having a little house of our own."

"You shall have plates and cups with your names on too," said Twinkle.

"How lovely!" said Fred. "We shall be just like pets."

"You will," said Twinkle. "We will look after you well, and not forget you at all."

They took the children to Fairyland. They showed them into a dear little house with two rooms. A good fire burned in one room, for it was cold. There were two beds in the bedroom, but they had only one blanket on each.

"We'll be cold with only one blanket," said Fred.

"Oh, we'll bring you more," said Twinkle.
"Now see – aren't these dear little cups and
plates and dishes – all with your names on!"

They certainly were nice. The children were
very pleased. They went into the garden of the
little house. It was wired all round, and there
was a gate, tall and strong, with a padlock on it.

"We'll lock you in, so that no bad brownie
or pixie can get you," said Twinkle. "Now
we'll just go and tell everyone you are here, and
then they can come and look at you through the
wire, and you can talk to them."

The first day was great fun, and the meals were delicious, served in the cups and dishes with their names on. But when night came, and the children went into the little house, they found that it was very cold.

The fire had gone out. There was no coal or wood to be seen. And dear me, Twinkle had forgotten to bring the extra blankets for their beds!

They shivered. "We'll call for Twinkle, or go and find him," said Eileen. So they called. But nobody came. They tried to open the gate, but it was locked. They went back to the cold house and hoped their little candle would last till the daylight came.

They were so cold that night, they couldn't sleep. The wind howled round. Eileen was thirsty, but she couldn't find any taps in the house at all.

She felt cross with Twinkle. "I do think he might look after us better," she said. "He promised to bring us warm blankets, and he didn't. And there isn't a drop of water to drink! After all, if he wants us to be like pets here, he ought to treat us well. We can't look after ourselves!"

The next day the children waited for Twinkle

to come. He came at last – but he didn't bring them much breakfast.

'I'll bring you a better dinner," he said. "What's that – you want a drink? All right, I'll bring that later. I'm rather busy at the moment. And yes – I'll bring those blankets. How stupid of me to forget!"

But he didn't come again that day. Other pixies came and stared through the fence, but as the gate was locked they could not get in to give the children any food or water. They grew angry and frightened.

Twinkle came about six o'clock. "So sorry not to have been able to come before," he said. "I had such a lot to do. Oh dear – I've forgotten the water again – and the blankets. Still, here is some bread and butter. I'll go back for the other things."

"Only bread-and-butter," said the poor children, who were now dreadfully hungry. "Oh dear! Bring us something else, please. And we think we'd like to go home tomorrow."

Twinkle went off. He didn't come back that night! Eileen and Fred were so thirsty that they cried. They didn't undress because they were too cold. They sat huddled on their beds, feeling miserable.

"It's raining," said Eileen. "Let's go out and open our mouths to drink the rain – then we shall get a drink."

They did – but they also got soaked through which made them colder than ever. There was still no fire, because Twinkle had forgotten to bring them wood or coal. The candle had burnt out. It was dark and horrid in the little house, which could have been so cosy and comfortable.

"I don't call this being pets!" sobbed Eileen. "We're forgotten. They don't love us a bit – they don't remember to give us water or proper food, or to keep us warm. They don't deserve to have us as pets!"

Fred was quiet for a moment. Then he spoke in a serious voice. "Eileen – I think the pixies have done this on purpose! This is how we keep our pets! We forget to give them proper food –we forget to give them fresh water – we don't clean out their cages when we should – and you know we didn't give poor old Rover any warm straw in his kennel those cold nights."

"Oh," said Eileen. "Oh, poor Rover! Fred, I know what it feels like now, don't you, to be in a cage, not able to look after ourselves or get food – and then to be forgotten. It's dreadful.

It's wrong. I'll never do such a thing again. I'll always love my pets and look after them."

As soon as she said that a strange thing happened. She felt warm and cosy and comfortable – and as she felt round, she gave a loud cry.

"Fred! I'm not in that little house – I'm in my own bed at home! How did it happen?"

They never knew how it was that they had gone from Fairyland to their own beds, and I don't know either – all I know is that as soon as they had learnt their lesson, they were back home again.

They didn't forget what they had felt like when they had been forgotten pets in Fairyland. They love their pets now, and care for them well. It was a good idea of Twinkle's, wasn't it, to make them into pets, and then pretend to forget them.